GARRET DIMPLE

AND THE SONG OF

THE

SALMON GIRL

DAN A. REID

ORIGINAL WRITING

978-1-907179-88-4

A cip catalogue for this book is available from the National Library.

Published by Original Writing Ltd., Dublin, 2010.

Printed by Cahill Printers Limited, Dublin.

Dedicated to my late parents,

Sarah and Myles Reid

*And to Mary Sweeney who thought the story was
"Magical"*

Contents

CHAPTER 1

When Sammy leapt up and broke through the sloping field, the other children stood up and began to question why. Ignoring their shouts, he was lost in a desperate run that only he understood just then. Already their voices were becoming fainter as his mind went over the reasons for his panic, and as he stumbled and then bounded headfirst into the centre of the field where the children lost sight of him beneath a forest of long grasses, he lost all awareness of where they were and could no longer even hear them calling. In his rush through the high stinging grasses, his only sense of direction was in his mind; the way ahead was a jungle of bowing gold-green stems that he smashed through without pause or thought for any danger that may lie in wait. The stump of an ailing oak tree to the side of the field and just visible over the grasses was his only reference point. Even in his sweaty rush he had somehow, without much thought, worked out that if he ran parallel to it he would reach that place where he needed to be. Yet such were the undulations in the ground that he at times lost sight of the tree and strayed from following a straight path to one which had a series of deviations and s-shapes and these made his run longer.

Behind him, the other children, Louise and Padraig, shared a confusion that neither of them had been prepared for. They were still in that dappled place where the Greenback River tumbled over a last weir and swirled in bubbling eddies before it spread out to course on towards the town of Creel.

"Lou, what did you say to him?" came Padraig's terse question as he realized that Sammy's obvious panic was no joke.

"Nothing! I said nothing. I just," answered Louise, perplexed and trying to remember.

"What?"

"I just told him that I saw his sister Dervla and her friend Maeve playing up near Lushly Fields."

Padraig's mouth dropped. "Lushly Fields? That's why he's run off!"

"I don't understand."

"Before you got here, Sammy and I were down at Passer's Bridge," explained Padraig. "We overheard two men from Creel talking. They'd been fishing but had caught nothing. You've heard all the talk in the town about there being no fish in any of Lissendel's rivers. Well, it's true! There are no fish! According to the two men there's some curse stopping the fish coming to our shores, and the rivers are all empty. And they said that the curse is even making the crops fail and that before long it would cause a great famine throughout Lissendel."

"But what has that got to do with Sammy running off like that?" interrupted Louise.

Padraig continued, "They said that the only way the curse can be lifted is by someone called the Salmon Girl singing her song."

"Yes—but—" Louise tried to interrupt again but was stopped by Padraig.

"But nobody knows where the Salmon Girl is," he said impatiently. "Only that she has the most amazing singing voice. The little people have been searching high and low for her—"

"You mean, the fairies?"

"Yes. They say that there's a huge fairy rath beneath Lushly Fields. It's where they stay. They depend on the fish coming to our rivers and shores and the harvest of the crops as much as we do, and they know that the only way the curse can be lifted is if the Salmon Girl sings her song. But they don't know where she is. So they've been taking young girls who can sing from all over Lissendel, thinking that one of them might just have that special gift of a voice that makes her the Salmon Girl."

Finally, Louise saw sense. "And Sammy's sister, Dervla, is a wonderful singer! And now Sammy's gone to Lushly Fields to warn her?"

"Yes!" exclaimed Padraig, already moving away. "And we should go and help him!"

Without further question or explanation, the two of them took off after Sammy, racing first down the grassy incline of the sloping field and then on into the tall grasses where they followed the path that had already been flattened by Sammy's run.

In Lushly Fields, Sammy's sister Dervla and her friend Maeve were unaware of the commotion that was going on. They ran out to the centre of the field, carefree and sprightly, throwing an old cow-skin ball to each other. Dervla singing vivaciously with a near immaculate soprano voice: *I'm a Princess, a Princess, a Princess*, to which Maeve replied in a gravely, baritone bawl: *And I'm a Queen, I'm a Queen, I'm a Queen*. Laughing all the while, one of them would throw the ball while the other executed a majestic, if exaggerated, leap to catch it. Each time the ball went back and forth they laughed longer and louder, as they both tried to outdo the other by adding comedic antics and variations to their original leaps and catches. At no time, however, were they aware that all the while in the heat of their play that they were moving closer to a most treacherous and forbidden area of the field where unearthly forces had already prepared a binding welcome.

Even their play gave them an indication that all was not as it should be, for every time they threw the ball to each other it seemed to hang in the air for longer than the time before. Yet they failed to heed this as a warning and argued that the ball's sudden and unusual airborne properties, that hadn't been there a short time before, was just a result of it either being thrown too high or of it being caught up in some abnormal, fast stream of air where it was carried aloft by the wind.

"You're throwing it too high, Maeve!" complained Dervla, moving ever nearer to the fairy rath in her efforts to catch the ball.

Maeve laughed, replying, "I'm not. It's the wind."

"How come I can't get it to go as high as you can then?"

"I don't know. You're probably just facing the wrong direction to catch the wind. Or maybe you're not throwing it properly. Watch the way I throw it!"

When Maeve threw the ball again it was much higher than before. It floated on a swirling current of air that carried it above Dervla's head and out over the hedgerows in a series of loops and dips until it reached an area over the far end of the field where some blackthorn bushes fell away into a dark depression amongst a small circle of hills. There, it fell abruptly, bouncing silently at first on a worn grassless area, before rolling on a little further and then coming to a halt.

"Ah, Maeve," complained Dervla, running after the ball. "You're doing it on purpose, and it's not the wind!"

"I promise I'm not! And don't go up there, Dervla!" warned Maeve suddenly as an uneasy feeling that she was unable to explain took hold of her.

"The ball won't get itself, silly," replied Dervla as she continued on.

"But there's a fairy rath up there, you eegit!"

"A fairy rath? You don't believe all that now, do you?" laughed Dervla, as she reached the hedgerow.

"It's a fairy fort! It's where they live!"

"Well then, they won't want our ball crashin' in on them, will they?"

"Just leave it, please, Dervla!"

"I don't see any fort," answered Dervla, "just a few hills. And anyway, I don't believe in fairies."

"They're as real as anything," shouted Maeve, chasing after her. "The hills are the fairy fort!"

When Sammy reached the far end of the overgrown field, he crossed over a shallow ditch of wild prickly shrubs, then an embankment that was full of stinging nettles, and then a thin bridge over a rainwater frog-pond where he finally climbed over a fence into Lushly Fields.

"Sammy! Sammy! Wait!" called Louise and Padraig from far behind as they emerged from the long grasses and gained ground on him, but he was too engrossed in his race to get to the two girls to wait for them. Further on they could see Dervla and Maeve moving across the upper part of Lushly Fields to where a dark patch of foliage sank off into a hollow and a mound of small hills rose. Dervla was out in front and Maeve following a short way behind. Sammy was running after them frantically waving his hands in the air and shouting their names, but his efforts were in vain. His sister, Dervla, had already gone too far into that part of the field where the danger lay, and even though she could hear him shouting something, she couldn't quite make out what he was saying, as his voice seemed to lose its resonance in the big open field.

Dervla was still ignoring Maeve's warning too, and continuing on. "Well, I don't see any fairies or anyone else for that matter," she said boldly. "I see our ball though. It's in the middle of those little hills, near the bushes."

"Leave it, Dervla! It's bad luck to go in there!"

"It will be okay, Maeve. I'm only gettin' our ball back," retorted Dervla, already moving to the centre of the little hills where she proceeded to pick up the ball.

Maeve panicked. "Get out quickly before something happens!"

Dervla, however, ambled as slowly as she could as if to make the point to Maeve that she was unafraid. She looked out over the fields dreamily and then climbed one of the hills in the circle. It's beautiful here, she thought. From where she stood she could see the sunlight glistening on the Greenback River as it wound its way past the Treefellwells Hills and further off, all the roads that led to and from Creel, some with specks of movement that would have been townsfolk and travellers going about their business. Further off still, and pasted against a vast blue and orange sky, were the Winterlan Mountains and the dark forest there, over which a flock of birds were gathering as if to go on a great migration. To the south, she could see a darker sky spreading across from the east. She knew it would eventually come over the full extent of the sea and cover it from where it touched the sky on the horizon to where the tide broke before the grey cliffs by the shore. It was a subtle shadow that would gently bring the night. For a moment as she looked out at the vast splendour of it all, she thought that if the fairies did live in that place, it would be for the view.

"It's lovely up here, Maeve. Come on up," she said.

"No!"

"You can see everything."

"I don't care," protested Maeve. "Now come down, or I'm going."

"Go, if you want," answered Dervla derisively.

"I'm going, and I hope the fairies do get you!"

As Maeve marched back across the field, she heard Dervla calling to her. She would have ignored her and continue on had it not been for the strange tone in her voice and the question that followed.

"Maeve, do you hear it?" asked Dervla, listening as she looked in wonderment around her.

"Hear what?"

"The music. Can you not hear it?"

"Music? There's no music—"

"It's the harp and the fiddle and the pipes, playin'."

"I can't hear a thing."

"Come up here, and you'll hear it," said Dervla.

"If you're trying to trick me into going up there, it's not going to work, Dervla!"

"You know, it makes me want to...dance...and dance...and dance," answered Dervla as she spun like a ballerina.

Maeve still wasn't convinced that Dervla could hear music and truly believed that she was just trying to trick her into going up into the fairy fort. "I'm going home!" she shouted abruptly, as she began to walk away.

"Listen, it's getting louder!" cried Dervla.

Only then did Maeve hear what she thought were the pipes playing. At first, there was just a singular pristine note with a tone that was somehow sad and lonely. It rose with a spiralling call only to fall again to the point of almost fading away. Then, following a pause, the same haunting note rose again, only to be joined this time by another and another and another, until a most vibrant and magical sound filled the air. As the music gained resonance, it seemed that that one lonely note, still heard above all the others, had become a focus point around which there had gathered a concoction of every sound of every musical instrument that could be imagined. In seconds, it had exploded into a magnificent crescendo of sounds of extraordinary proportions. It was as if it was leading somewhere tremendous or celebrating a wonderful event. Quickly, Maeve turned to Dervla but panicked when she saw her dancing backwards into the gaping mouth of an amphitheatre, which was really an enormous dark hollow that had opened up in the hills around her.

"Dervla! Dervla! Watch out!" she screamed. "Behind you! Run! Run now! Watch out!"

Dervla, enchanted by the music, was unaware of what was happening. She could see Maeve running towards her and then Sammy and Louise and Padraig coming to join her. Still dancing and somehow never wanting to stop, she watched as they waved to her frantically. She could see too that they were shouting something to her, but she was unable to hear what it was, because the music had become so loud. Imprisoned by the wondrous lilting harmonies, she was the sole inhabitant of a lost world that was spinning through a vast endless space. She just kept dancing and dancing and moving deeper and deeper into the hollow, which she was still unaware of, until it was too late and it had closed around her. In just one moment and the passing of one to another, she was no more to be seen. The ball was all that was left among the circle of hills.

For some minutes after, the children ran back and forth not knowing what to do. At first, there was a stunned silence amongst them, and then all of them started to talk at once. Maeve started to walk away in disbelief at what had just happened. She was blaming herself for saying that she hoped that the fairies took Dervla, and yet she knew that she never really meant for it to happen. Sammy began to explain to Louise and Padraig what he had seen. He was arguing for going up to the very spot from where Dervla had disappeared and for trying to find an entrance into the hollow, until them both, after much argument, convinced him that the best thing to do was to go back to Creel for help.

CHAPTER 2

E ven before the children reached the road that wound its way into Creel, they began to run and shout. "They've taken her! They've got Dervla O'Sullivan! The fairies have! Up at Lushly Fields! They've taken her!"

Although they were running and shouting, the news seemed to go before them such was the amount of people coming and going. As they hurried through the rambling town's old quarters, the locals had already begun to gather outside their houses. Others came to their windows and doors wondering what all the fuss was about. Some of them too, had seen it all before. Sammy could hear them whispering, saying how terrible it was that the young girl had been taken and how there was little chance of her being given back. Again, he fought with the idea of just going back to Lushly Fields on his own to try to rescue Dervla but, remembering Louise's and Padraig's argument against this, decided that their suggestion to seek help in Creel made the most sense. He remembered hearing a story when he was younger about a young girl who had been taken by the fairies. At the time, it was just a story that meant nothing to him and that he never really believed, one that his mother Marcella, used to tell to him and Dervla to keep them from straying too far from Creel. It was about a butcher's daughter named Colleen who became charmed by the fairies and wandered off through the fields on a May evening and was never seen again. A note on her bedside table said that she had gone to meet the little people. When her family tried to rescue her, they were taken too. None of them were ever seen again. Sammy shrank from the thought that he would never see his sister Dervla again. In a fit of anger, he started running through the streets going from one person to another in the hope that one of them would have a favourable answer. "The fairies have my sister, Dervla! Can you help me get her back? Please! I mean, we can get her back...can't we?"

Some of the people looked away, and some shook their heads, while others threw their eyes to the ground with grim, downcast, and hopeless expressions on their faces. One by one, they dispersed as quickly as they had gathered, ghosting away down side streets, sidestepping into shops and public houses, or going back inside their own homes where they closed their windows and doors. After the streets had completely emptied, Sammy, left alone, realized just how helpless the situation was.

When he arrived at his house, Maeve, traumatized by all that had happened, was trying to tell his parents everything at once. "We were playing, just throwing a ball, just a ball," she said tearfully, "and the hills just...and I didn't know what to do... and there was this music...and then Dervla—"

"You're making no sense, Maeve," intervened Sammy's Mother, Marcella, while shaking her head to ward off a more aggressive demand to know what happened from her husband, Joe who was pacing the floor nearby. "Now calm down and tell us exactly what happened."

Maeve gulped a deep breath and wept as she recounted the story. "We were playing up at Lushly Fields, and our ball went into the fairy rath, the fort. I told Dervla not to go after it, but she wouldn't listen. But then she heard the fairy music, Marcella. I couldn't hear it at first, but then I did...just for a second. At least I think I did. Dervla could hear it all the time though. She was even dancin' to it. I told her it was dangerous up there, but it was too late! She just kept dancin' and dancin'...and then—"

"And then what?" demanded Sammy's father Joe as Maeve hesitated.

"The whole hillside opened up and swallowed her! It was the fairies! They've taken her! They've taken Dervla. I told her not to go there, Marcella! I promise I did!"

"Oh no, this can't happen to me, to us!" sobbed Marcella. "Not my pretty little one, Dervla! They can't have her! I won't let them!"

"You don't really expect us to believe this now, do you?" said Joe flippantly, his face glowing with unbelief and suspicion.

"I'm tellin' the truth!" cried Maeve.

"She's not lyin'," added Sammy, cowering a little from his father's gaze. "I saw it with my own eyes."

His father was not convinced however, and spoke through his feigned laughter. "You saw the fairies taking our Dervla?"

"I didn't see any fairies, but I saw the hole opening up in the hillside and closing around her."

"Now we're getting somewhere. Dervla fell down a hole, isn't that right?"

"We heard some men who were fishing near Passer's Bridge talking about how there were no fish coming to any of Lissendel's rivers or shores and about the crops failing. They said that it was happening because of a curse that had been put on all of Lissendel by an evil wizard from the north and the only way it could be lifted was if someone called the Salmon Girl would sing her special song, but nobody knew where she was. They said that the fairies know the special song but that even they don't know where the Salmon Girl is. They'd been taking any young girl with a good singing voice, like Dervla has, in the hope that she could sing the song."

"Fairies? A curse? A wizard? And now a Salmon Girl? Oh, and a special song? Stop all this nonsense now!"

Marcella snapped at her husband's dismissal of Sammy's story. "Where is our Dervla then, Joe? Where? Tell me?"

"She's fallin' down a hole. Maybe it's an old mineshaft. I'll get her back, don't worry," he answered, but the uncertain look in his eyes gave her no assurance that he would.

"If the fairies have taken her, you'll need help and help again and the kind of help that you can't just get from just anyone around here...except one or two," came a voice from a pale, shadowy face of a woman who appeared in the doorway. It was Biddy (known locally as *Biddy-the-witch*) a friend of Marcella's, who had been on her way home from the town's vegetable market when she heard the commotion.

"Oh would you go away, you old hag, and leave us alone. Can you not see that Marcella's upset?" rasped Joe.

"Old hag?" repeated Biddy, as she turned abruptly to go.

."No, don't go, please!" pleaded Marcella suddenly. "He didn't mean it...I mean...to call you a hag. He's just upset, like me. You're not a hag, Biddy. You've always been a good friend to us."

"I only wanted to help," answered Biddy, hurt, "and he calls me a hag."

"Can you help us, Biddy?" wept Marcella before turning to her husband Joe with a fierceness in her eyes that suddenly made him want to apologize to Biddy.

"Please," he said, before adding remorsefully. "I didn't mean to call you a...I just didn't mean it."

"Of course, I'll help you," smiled Biddy to Marcella with new enthusiasm, while still staring at Joe with a steely rebuke.

"Put a curse on the fairies, Biddy!" shouted Sammy.

"There's an idea, Biddy," said Marcella. "Put a curse on the whole lot of them! Make them regret the very day that they laid a finger on an O'Sullivan!"

"Put a curse on the little people, and it will come back ten times on yourself," answered Biddy, sharply. "No. We'll find another way of dealing with them."

"What do they want with her?" Marcella cried despairingly.

Suddenly Biddy's eyebrows arched with fright. "I hope it's not the Amadawn who has her."

"A curse on him if he has!" snarled Marcella, as she roused the others. "Come on! There's no time to lose!"

"Will you give up on the curses, Marcella? I told you we'd find another way of dealing with them, and we will get Dervla back... but never through the use of a curse. Understand?"

Biddy was still talking when Marcella, Joe, and Sammy started to leave the house to go up to Lushly Fields. On the road outside, Sammy's friends Louise and Padraig joined them. Then Biddy, realizing that she was being left behind, ran after them. The only one left when they had all gone was Maeve who said quietly to herself, "You'll all be taken—every last one of you. You'll all be chained up in the black pits of that fairy rath and lost forever."

At Lushly Fields Sammy showed them all the very spot from where Dervla had been taken. "I was just standing there down the field when I saw the whole hillside opening up like a great big mouth, and then Dervla just disappearing into it."

"Well I don't see any hole anywhere?" answered his father, searching around.

"It was right there up that hill."

Immediately, Marcella ran forward to the hill. "If there's anyone listening in there?" she shouted. "You've taken my daughter, Dervla O'Sullivan, and I want her back right now! Do you hear?"

"They can hear you all right," said Biddy. "They hear all of us all of the time, even when we're whispering or a million miles away."

"If you don't give her back by midnight," threatened Marcella suddenly, "I'll have a curse put on this rath and everyone who lives here until the end of time!"

"It's no use, Marcella," said Biddy. "They're not afraid of us."

"Even if I have to call up the dark forces to do it, I'll get our Dervla back," continued Marcella.

"Stop it now!" exclaimed Biddy. "The dark forces don't frighten them. You should know that, Marcella. Some of them even serve the dark forces."

"What are the dark forces?" whispered Louise to Padraig.

Padraig stuttered. "The d-devil and his furies, I think."

A short time after, as if in response to Marcella's threat, a creeping darkness began to come down on everything around. Suddenly, she began to feel faint. She was losing all hope of ever seeing Dervla again, and perhaps that was the cause of her weakness, she thought. Joe went to help her, but even he had a feeling of weakness unlike anything that he had ever experienced before. Quietly, he was worried that if they didn't leave there soon before it got really dark, they would be at the mercy of terrible things, things that he had heard spoken of in the town, things, he remembered, that had caused raised eyebrows, gulped breaths, and palpitations in those that spoke of them. He had never dwelt on those terrible things before then, or really ever gave them any credence, but in the fading light, they grew as ominous in his mind as the shadows that were beginning to overwhelm the place where they stood.

"I don't like this," wailed Biddy, sensing that something unusual was happening around them.

Sammy's eyes grew wild. "It-it-it's too-too early for it to get this dark," he stuttered.

"I think we better get going now!" said Joe as he shakily pulled Marcella back from the fairy rath.

Just then, they became aware that all around there was a sweeping hush. The birdcalls that had been abundant just a short time before and that had always been a part of that place fell silent as quickly as the light had declined. Then the wind stirred, and the clouds gathered, mixing a murky soup of greyness and blackness into a huge swollen fist that weighed down on the land with an irresistible and unyielding heaviness. Instantly, the skies rolled with thunder and cracked open with yellow ribbed streaks of lightning that came to ground in jagged forks. The wind began to blow fiercely too, wrapping black thunderclouds into violent vortices that swept down the full length of Lushly Fields and then around Biddy and the children with such tenacious ferocity that they could no longer hold their footing. Losing all control of their movements in the ferocious squalls, they were pushed, harried and bounded along towards a wind-battered hedgerow at the side of the field. The rains came then in endless grey sheets, as if to press them back and to make them huddle. Nearby, Joe and Marcella found shelter under some giant creaking oak trees, but even there, they could not escape the storm's rage. Thrashing harder and harder, it forced the trees to bend over, causing some of their branches to snap and fall. Everything was askew in the torrential downpour that followed, and as the angry wind tugged and tossed and lifted up and threw down, it only seemed to grow stronger and stronger.

The voices of the soaked and dishevelled group were lost against the roar of the storm, but still their cries went up.

"We can't stay here!" roared Padraig. "It's too dangerous!"

"It'll be worse, if we're caught out in the open," warned Louise.

"Biddy, do something!" shouted Sammy.

"Do what?" answered Biddy.

"I don't know. Do whatever witches do. Just do it now! Make the wind stop!"

"I can't make the wind stop! Besides, it's not just any wind!"

"We're all going to die, if you don't do something soon!" pleaded Padraig.

"It's them, isn't it, who are causing it to happen – the fairies?" said Louise.

At that same moment the silhouette of a man appeared on another hill to one side of the field. Biddy was first to see him but could hardly believe her eyes. "I don't believe it," she said to herself in wonderment, moving out into the open. Moments after, the others, questioning her sudden movement away from the hedgerows, saw what she was looking at, but they were unsure if there was someone actually there or whether it was just a trick of the bad light. What they saw was the dark image of a man wearing a long hooded cloak and carrying a large blackthorn staff. It seemed that he was unaffected by the wind even though it was gusting at its greatest might all around him.

"It can't be him," said Biddy then, still looking at the man in bewilderment.

"Who is it?" asked Marcella. "What's he up to?"

"It is him, by god!" replied Biddy.

"Who is he?" enquired Sammy.

"Whoever he is, he's in for it now. Look at the size of those clouds coming down," said Padraig, as a swirling black mass of cloud enveloped the hillside and that whole end of Lushly Fields.

"We're all doomed," cried Louise.

As the bloated clouds tumbled over the field, Biddy and the others ducked low for cover. Only Sammy remained to witness what happened. Spellbound, he watched the strange man standing out on the hill, his long cloak pushed back and his face glowing with determination. He was talking or shouting something towards the sky that Sammy couldn't hear. All of the time, the storm was bearing down on him, its clouds twisting into dark grotesque shapes that belched out jagged shafts of lightning and spat them down. The man was unaffected though. Lifting his staff, he pointed it at the main belly of the fat menacing clouds, again shouting something, a command of some sort. Sammy had begun to question the man's sanity. Only someone who had lost his mind or who had had too much to drink would stand out on an exposed hill in such a storm, shouting at the sky. But when a bolt of lightning bigger than any that had been produced by the storm came from the man's staff and entered the clouds, he was suddenly filled with awe and knew that the man was neither drunk nor insane. In the moments that followed, the clouds were quickly dispersed and then sucked away into nothing, allowing light to brighten the field again and to spread over the hill.

"Did-did-did-did-did you see-see that? Did you?" he asked the others as they emerged from under the trees.

Biddy was already dancing around with delight. "What a man! What a man! What a man!"

"Who is he?" wondered Louise.

"He's disappeared! Where's he gone to?" gasped Padraig.

Marcella and Joe were last to come out from the shelter of the trees and had seen nothing of what happened. "Who are they talking about, Biddy?" Marcella asked.

"The storm's gone anyway," remarked Joe.

Sammy stood back and punched the air. "He must be a great warlock!"

Biddy turned to them. "His name's Garret Dimple, and he's an extraordinary individual, simple in nature but complicated too. He's not a warlock but a wizard perhaps, although there are no words that can truly describe him and what he can do. He's a natural wonder, a wonderful freak! Some say he's even a ghost."

"What? A real ghost?" asked Sammy.

"He's no ghost, just a man, a simply wonderful man."

Chapter 3

That evening, Sammy sat down in his room and tried to work out what to do next. He noticed that since they had returned from Lushly Fields, his mother and father had hardly said a word. He knew also, that his father Joe still harboured doubts about the whole affair and before long would convince his mother to doubt all that happened too. After all, it was easier to accept a more rational explanation for Dervla going missing than that of her being taken by the fairies. They still expected her to come walking through the door at any moment with some story about how she had played a joke on all of them by pretending to be taken by the fairies up at Lushly Fields. And he was sure that they would even find some convincing explanation for the clearly unnatural storm that they had experienced when there earlier. They were sheltering during the worst of it and missed the magic that Garret Dimple used to quell its terrible winds. If even the wizard, he thought, had remained around after the storm they might have been more open to believe, but as quickly as the winds died so, too, was he gone. Regardless of what his parents believed, he knew what really happened, and being so close to stopping it but not succeeding gave him a dreadful feeling of hopelessness that he knew would stay with him until he got his sister Dervla back home safely again.

Outside, he could hear a last blackbird whistling as the skies closed over with night. It was a high, lone sound that echoed out across the darkening valleys, hills and fields as if to connect them all with that one solitary cry. As he looked out across the deepening skyline where stars were blinking into life, his attention spun for a second when a falling star skimmed off the rim of the sky just above his window. It made him wonder if somewhere Dervla could see it too, or if she could see the other stars or hear the blackbird's whistle. Even the thought of those small connections was enough to give him comfort. At the back of his mind, though, were the fears that she may be under a strange and different sky that had no stars and no birdcalls. As he pondered her whereabouts, he sent his thoughts out across the night in the hope that they would somehow find her and bring her comfort. Before long, he was drifting with those same thoughts, travelling over the dark landscape of Lissendel, slipping ever away into a cocoon of sleep where a dream began to unfold.

"Sammy," called the voice in his dream. "Where are you, Sammy?"

"Is that you, Dervla?" he asked, trying to look through the smoky veil of his sleep.

"Help me," pleaded the voice.

Then somehow he found himself approaching the place where the voice came from. He was straining to see who it was, but all he could make out was a shadow of a girl - that looked like his sister - on a strange twisting road.

"Dervla, is that you?" he asked again.

"Please come back to Lushly Fields and take me home. Sammy...Sammy...Sammy," cried the voice as the dream began to fade. Several times after, the voice made the same requests before it finally trailed off and the dream ended.

"Wait!" cried Sammy, as he jumped up from his sleep. He had expected to see someone there before him, but soon realized that he was alone. As seconds went by, he began to think back on the dream and to try to figure out what it meant, but he was unable to make any sense of it. Then, as if he had suddenly returned once more to its slumbering depths, he heard his name being called again. "Sammy...Sammy, are you awake?"

Yes, he told himself. I am awake. Then he realized that the voice was not the one from his dream. It was another girl's voice, a familiar one, and it was coming from somewhere outside his bedroom window where the morning light had already spread all over the land. Instantly, he dashed to the window and saw that it was Maeve outside.

"You've got to come," she said with a breathless urgency in her voice. "It's Dervla. She's come back! I had a dream about her. It said to go back to Lushly Fields to take her home. I was on my way there just now when I found her wandering back along the road."

A rush of excitement filled Sammy. "Where is she now?"

"She's out the road! I think there's something wrong with her though. She's not herself. I can't get her to come home."

Sammy delayed no time in dashing downstairs and running from the house. In minutes, he was following Maeve to a crossroads where Dervla, her face paler than he had ever seen it before, stood alone. It was as if she was a stranger to that place (one that Sammy knew she had been to many times before and that she should have known well) and was preoccupied with the decision as to what road to take. Still Sammy was delighted to have her back, but when he went to tell her this, she leisurely brushed him aside and walked on down the winding road that led away from Creel and back towards Lushly Fields.

"She can't want to go back to the fairy rath, can she?" asked Sammy.

"I told you she's not herself. They must have done something to her," answered Maeve. "It's like she's asleep or something."

"Dervla!" shouted Sammy, taking her by the arm. "Wake up! We're taking you home."

As they started on the road back to Creel, all was well in Sammy's mind, and already he was anticipating the welcome that his parents would give them when they got home. Maeve, however, had suspicions that all was not as it should be, and when Dervla began hissing and growling with malicious intent, she knew that her reservations had been right.

"S-S-Sammy," Maeve stuttered, "I t-think you s-should let go of D-Dervla's arm."

"What? Why?" was Sammy's absentminded reply before he too, saw the snarling creature at his side and jumped with fright to immediately release her arm. "You're not Dervla!"

"You're not Dervla!" repeated the creature whose face had changed to that of a malevolent hag. "No. I'm not Dervla. I'm the poor forsaken one. That's me. Take me or leave me! I'm all you're getting!"

Sammy gasped. "Where is she? Where's my sister, Dervla?"

"She's probably boiling in a pot by now, or roasting in an oven, or sizzling over a fire!" laughed the hag, spitefully.

From somewhere Sammy found the strength to issue a threat but knew that it had no real substance when his words faltered. "If she's harmed in any way...I'll...we'll...all of the people in Creel will..."

"Run for cover!" sniggered the creature, finishing his sentence. "The good people of Creel are nothing more than a lot of snivelling buffoons who are really only interested in themselves. They won't help you. Ha! Ha! Ha!"

"We'll keep you prisoner!" said Sammy finally mustering a proper threat.

Slowly the hag came forward towards Sammy, her threatening eyes staring unblinkingly at his as she croaked, "I don't think so! I really, really don't think so!"

The warning in her voice was not lost on Sammy, but he knew that if he backed down just then that it would only further serve the interests of the hag, so instead he countered her fearsome gabble with another threat. "We'll call a great wizard down on you to bind you up with his magic so that you'll never escape until the end of time!"

"What wizard?"

"Eh, he's a...great wizard, a grand master...of wizardry," answered Sammy, unable to remember the wizard's name in his panic. "He even stopped the fairy wind up at Lushly Fields!"

"What's his name?"

"His name's...Garret. Garret's his name!"

"Just Garret?" remonstrated the hag, insincerely. "That's such a lonely name, don't you think?"

Sammy was looking to Maeve for help, but she shook her head to say that she couldn't remember the full name either. "Garret's his name!" he said again boldly but was surprised when another voice came from behind.

"Garret Dimple!" exclaimed the voice.

Instantly, the hag jumped to attention and with a trailing hand clattered Sammy across the forehead with such force that it sent him reeling off to one side. Even drowsy, he saw that the owner of the voice was none other than Garret Dimple himself and felt relieved when the wizard casually intercepted another assault on him from the hag, holding his staff out while shouting, "Not so fast!"

When Maeve went to help Sammy back to his feet, they both laughed when they saw how the hag, hissing and disgruntled, had been left suspended in mid-air, her legs dangling and askew as if ready to run but really unable to go anywhere. Neither of them saw what Garret did to make this happen, nor did the hag. There was no shot or bolt or flash, just an invisible force that somehow Garret, with minimal effort, had brought to bear on the miserable creature to leave her hanging there with nowhere to go.

"One minute she was my sister, Dervla," recounted Sammy, as he took a closer look at the snarling hag, "and the next she turned into this...creature."

Garret's voice went deep with warning. "This one was never your sister. She's a changeling, sent by the fairies to replace your sister. If you had brought her to your home she would have caused endless trouble. Changelings have unquenchable thirsts and hungers that can never be satisfied. Before long she would have become an all consuming fiend, a monster that, when all the food in your house ran out, would begin to stalk your chickens and your sheep and your cattle until there was nothing left to eat but the very ones who had given her shelter!"

Sammy gulped as Maeve looked on with disbelief. "She'd eat us?"

"Down to the very bone!"

Both Maeve and Sammy stepped back such was the fear that came over them.

"What will we do with her?" Sammy asked.

"Will we ever get Dervla back, Mister Dimple?" added Maeve.

"Now listen," smiled Garret, his face awash with a mixture of empathy and guile. "You must leave some things to those who are meant to deal with them."

Sammy face screwed up inquisitively. "I don't understand."

"Your sister is far away by now. The fairy rath at Lushly Fields is merely a stopover for the little people, a station they use to watch what goes on above ground, one of many dotted throughout Lissendel. Dervla is probably being held in one of King Lugh's strongholds far to the north of the Winterlan Mountains. Then again she could be in one of his palaces down south. She could even be in one of his undersea hides or off on an island in the uncharted lands."

"We'll never get her back then, if we don't know where she is," surmised Sammy dejectedly.

"We can't give up, Sammy!" argued Maeve.

Garret put his arms around both of them then and drew them near. In his face and eyes, they saw something unworldly, a shining ardour that glowed with gentle warmth that brightened their own faces and gave them hope. Before he even said another word, their minds were adrift on an air of expectancy. "I'm here to help you," he said then. "When I said that you must leave some things to those who are meant to deal with them, I should have added, especially when those things have greater significance than they seem to have at first."

"I still don't understand," said Sammy.

"Do you know Linahen Rock?" asked Garret, his voice deep with mystery.

"It's near the Treefellwells Hills and not too far from where the Greenback River enters the sea," answered Sammy. "Some people in Creel say that it's haunted."

"Yes, everyone's afraid to go there," added Maeve. "It's supposed to be haunted by some giant. He comes on certain nights and is heard moaning and crying."

"They say that a leprechaun lives there too."

"Linahen Rock is a special place to be sure," smiled Garret, "and it will have its part to play when everything unfolds."

Sammy was intrigued but somewhat agitated too. "The fairies want Dervla to sing some special song that will make the fish swim again. Is that true?"

Garret's eyes were filled with a mixture of memories and concern when he spoke. "They call it the *Song of the Salmon*

Girl, and yes, it has that power to make the fish come back to our shores again. Dervla has the voice of an angel. That much can't be denied, but she could never in a million years master that special song. Only the one true Salmon Girl herself has the voice for that song. Only she can bring the fish home. Old King Lugh is a fool for taking your sister, and I'll tell him that to his face when I see him."

"When will you see him?"

"There's someone else I have to see first to point me in the right direction. I need to find out exactly where they're keeping Dervla."

"And this person will know that?"

"He'll know. Sure he's one of the king's own."

"He's one of the little people then?"

"Yes. He's the Leprechaun of Linahen Rock!"

"He'll tell you nothing but lies! Lies and more lies!" hissed the hag. "But I, the poor forsaken one, know how to make him tell the truth!"

Suddenly, Garret swung around to where the hag was, his face grim with threat. "And you're going to tell us, are you?"

The hag sniggered fiendishly then, knowing that Garret had no option but to bargain with her. "That depends...on how well you treat me, and I have to say you've made a bad start, leaving me dangling like this. I have needs, you know. I want my freedom, and I want...things, lots of things!"

"What things?"

"Well," she began, as her thoughts raced with things fantastic, "what would anyone want when they have nothing? I want everything! Everything, that is, that a normal everyday pretty girl would expect to have."

Garret raised his eyebrows to avoid giggling. "I don't know when it was that you last looked in a mirror but you're slightly off the mark when it comes to being a normal girl, let alone a pretty one."

"Don't make fun of me, Mister!" snapped the hag, her face wrinkled with fury. "That is, if you want to know what I know!"

"I just meant—"

"I know what you meant! Okay, I'm not what you would call normal, but that's not my fault. All I ever wanted was to be normal. Normal and pretty like a flower in a meadow. Instead, I'm like a blight on the landscape and an eyesore. But you know what, Mister – inside in my mind, sometimes, just sometimes, I see myself as a happy pretty girl with a normal life."

"Some things just aren't meant to be," answered Garret, as Maeve and Sammy turned away with laughter.

"What would you do if you were me, Mister, and you knew that you had some vital information that a certain wizard needed to know if he was going to make a sly-eyed, mean-mouthed and unmitigated liar of a leprechaun tell the truth?"

"You want to make a bargain for your freedom, is that it?"

"Of course I want my freedom," said the hag, her voice gloating with avarice as her eyes stared madly at a vision of her future that only she could see. "But there are also...other things that I want, that I need! Gold would be nice, jewels, too, and the finest clothes that money could buy. It would be nice to live in a mansion with servants tending to my every need. You know, someone to get me this and to get me that. Someone to get my coat and get my hat! Ha!"

"You really don't want much, do you?" remarked Garret derisively.

"Don't worry. You don't have to give me all the things that I want. You see, I'm sure I could get them all myself, if I just have one or two things to start with."

"Again I'm asking, what things?"

"Well, my freedom for one, that goes without saying. Then I was thinking that you being a magician and all, I mean a wizard...that you could make some improvements, little ones even, to...my face and body."

"What—?"

"Look at my face. Not a pretty sight, is it? And this body... all twisted and bent as it is. My legs have seen better days - and look, I've been given shovels for hands and paddles for feet! And let's face it, head-to-toe, I could do with less fat and more

23

bone structure. To put it lightly, I'm a real horror show! I know it and so do you. Now I want you to make the horror go away, Mister. I could be beautiful. I could...with a little magic. Make me pretty, Mister. Make me a beauty, a real beauty!"

"Make you beautiful?" laughed Garret. "I'm not a miracle worker!"

"You get what you want, if I get what I want! Now set me free!"

"And you expect me to trust you?"

"Green's his name, the Leprechaun of Linahen Rock," said the hag resolutely, "and a grumpier individual, although I do find him strangely attractive, you won't find anywhere in the whole of Lissendel! There, I've given you something, now let me down out of this whatever-it-is contraption that you've trapped me in."

"And how do we make this Green tell the truth?"

"I'll tell you that when you release me!"

Garret thought for a moment, but his eyes were already filled with the action he was about to take. Turning with sudden violent movements that made the others cower with fright, he drew his staff and wielded it through the air in a great clockwise arc that sent vicious fiery ropes spiralling away across the fields. Suddenly, the hag, cowering after the fierceness of Garret's actions, found that she had been freed.

"Any of your tricks and I'll fry you where you stand!" warned Garret.

"But I'm free to go where I want?"

"Yes, but—"

"There'll...there'll be no tricks. No, no tricks from me," she answered timidly. "Now come on, turn me into a head turner, a real beauty!"

"That's easier said than done!" complained Garret, before reconsidering when he saw the hag's eyes filling with tears. "Ok, ok! But not until Green tells me where the king is holding the girl. Now, you tell me what I need to know to make him!"

"He likes his gold, does Green."

"Show me a leprechaun who doesn't."

"But there's something he values even more. I've seen him disappear on moonlit nights at Linahen Rock, and I've heard him cry out with a horrible squeal as if the demons from the pits of hell had come for him!"

"We all have our bad days," quipped Garret.

The hag's face turned sour with indignation. "You don't understand! He can call the dead to life and make them do his bidding! He lets out his cry and the dead rise."

"What cry?"

"*Phoulardnacrushnaparteenthomond!*"

Something stirred in Garret's mind when the hag said this and a small tremor ran the length of his spine. He knew of many such powerful and potent words but had always been cautious when it came to their use, for sometimes their influence was unbounded and had unseen repercussions for those that used them.

"It's his great secret. That's for sure," continued the hag, "and it holds some great meaning for him. Green knows everything that goes on in the king's palaces. He'll know where they've taken the girl, but you won't get any truth out of him unless you have something special to bargain with."

"I'll bargain with him!" growled Garret angrily, while tightly wielding his staff.

"You won't frighten him easily. But if he thought that you could cast a spell that would strike him dumb, so that he could never again utter, '*Phoulardnacrushnaparteenthomond!*' he might see sense and tell you what you need to know."

"How come you know so much about Green?"

The hag huffed. "Before I was a changeling, King Lugh gave me a job in which I had to pretend to be the Salmon Girl. You see he promised the whole kingdom underground that the Salmon Girl would sing her song and lift the curse on Lissendel, but when he heard that she had long gone missing he panicked. Immediately, he gave the order to snatch any young girl that could sing from all across Lissendel and then he set up the farce of me pretending to be the real Salmon Girl to stop all the talk that was going around about her having gone missing. My job was to be seen on the tides and on the shores around the coast and sometimes at Linahen Rock disguised as the Salmon Girl, but to never let anybody get so near as to see who I really was. It was at Linahen Rock one night that I heard Green saying his secret word and saw the power that it had. What he brought forth from underground put a terror into me that I've never experienced before or since! I tell you he has the power in his secret word to call up the dead."

"What exactly did you see?"

"A giant beast rose up in a grey mist and stood there before Green, his eyes as dark as the darkest night!"

"That's all?"

"I was too frightened to wait around there any longer. I ran away, and I kept running till I was as far away from there as I could get!"

Garret looked to Sammy and then to Maeve. Without uttering a word, they all simultaneously agreed that the hag was telling the truth and that her idea for persuading Green to tell Garret where Dervla was being held was a good one.

"*Phoulardnacrushnaparteenthomond*?" mused Garret, stroking his chin. For a short time he considered what to do next but then moved to a higher vantage point when his attention was taken by a strange play of light that slipped across the hills nearby with a creeping shadow. The sudden movement altered his train of thought, but his calculating mind returned to its considerations when brightness wrapped itself around the dark patch of sky and took away the shadow.

CHAPTER 4

As the hag slinked away across the fields anticipating how differently everybody would treat her when she was beautiful, Garret's eyes arched with faraway thoughts. He knew to be wary of certain places like Linahen Rock, where old ways harnessed great forces that came to bear with a vengeance on those who disturbed their sacred stillness or dared to unravel their secrets. And yet, as if some connection — that had been made long ago with that place but forgotten with the passing of time — had somehow been renewed, he felt himself inexorably drawn there.

He found himself remembering a story about another time not too long ago when there were also no fish swimming in Lissendel's rivers or to her shores. It told of a huge giant named Andale who, following a year of terrible drought in which his elderly parents fell ill and died, spent his time wandering the mountains and fields of Lissendel as if searching for something that he had lost. He was a kind-hearted soul who was born of normal-sized Lissendelian parents but who outgrew all those on Lissendel of his own age until he was no longer accepted as being one of them and even vilified as being a freak of nature. He loved to give help wherever it was needed, yet even those he helped treated him as though he was some outcast. During that terrible year of drought, the whole countryside was under threat from a dreadful darkness that brought down weather of all extremes. While there were the most violent lightning bolts that shook the earth and wild relentless thunderstorms that lasted for days, there was not one drop of rain. The land was slowly becoming a desert as increasingly as it was becoming deserted. Lissendelians were taking to boats and ships in their hundreds and thousands. Most of them fled to the sanctuary of the other islands of the continent of Tide, the sprawling landmass at the centre of all the charted islands, while some braved the vast open sea to search for the uncharted lands. In his mind, Garret imagined the sea taking Lissendel's young and old in its heaving embrace as if to play a game of chance with them, spitting some back from where they came, guiding others to safe shores, and pulling some other unfortunates down under to feed its deepest depths. In those times, it truly seemed that it was the sea that determined who would continue or who would cease to be. Lissendel's history could have stopped there and then, too, had it not been for the giant Andale and his searching for that which had been lost. No one knows for sure if it was an act of providence or some intractable element of chance that drew the lady from the sea and curious giant together, but it was said that when he was seen late one night at Linahen Rock in the company of the silken figure of that demure and ethereal female from the sea who was to sing a mystical song, that Lissendel's troubles ceased.

For all the stories told about the giant, and Lissendelians were a people who loved a good story, it was the one with this shadowy female, Garret remembered, that was the most repeated. As he began remembering how the story went — and the whole event was witnessed by a troop of little people who, having a vested interest in removing the threat that was hanging over the land at that time (the same one that was hanging over it again, thought Garret) passed the story on to certain *intuitive* Lissendelians, individuals such as *fairy doctors, white witches of the woods* and *those with the gifts of healing and prayer,* so that the whole event would be told over and over and never forgotten — he began to see it clearly in his mind's eye as if it was happening all over again.

It told of how, on a dewy moon-bleached night, Andale, lost in his wanderings, found a beautiful but sickly female on a mountain path where few people ever ventured. Thinking that she was at death's door he took her to a nearby cave and made her as comfortable as he possibly could, laying her down on a bed of mountain grasses and building a roaring fire of twigs and dried gorse to keep her warm. All the time, she was delirious with fever and muttering things he couldn't understand. One minute her voice would almost choke with panic and the next cackle with ungodly screams that sent small animals scurrying for cover. In a terrible tirade, words without meaning spilled out from her mouth, in a frantic, ungracious babble that made no sense until at last she uttered in a single lucid moment the words, *the sea, the sea, the sea...* That she repeated the same thing again and again with a crying desperation in her voice and tears in her eyes, while pointing out over the mountains towards where the sea lay, made him consider that it had an importance to her that just then he was at a loss to fathom. Yet at once he made it his quest to get her there, wrapping her in his own cloak and carrying her in his arms over the dangerous dark paths. Throughout the night he stumble and struggled, picking his way round and over the broken tracks, careful never to jolt or in any way disturb the sleeping angel in his arms, till at last a shore-breeze gushed at his face, and he saw the shining darkness of the sea.

It was there that new life came to the female, and she wafted from his arms into the sea's wash, easing his concern with a smile and a hand on his that gave him assurance that all was okay when he went to stop her. For some time he watched her wading out into the silken waters, her slight ghostly figure getting smaller against the sea's vastness the further she went away from where he stood, until at last she was gone completely from his sight. As a terrible panic grew in his chest, he started suddenly after her, calling, *"No! Come back! Come back!"* However his calls were short-lived and, he thought, for nobody when he began to consider that it all might have been a wonderful insane dream, manufactured by the long days of his solitary wanderings and the imaginings of his lonely mind. As he looked at the black sea where a dipping moon was resting on its own reflection, he began to doubt if the female had ever been there at all. Only when he turned to walk back from the shore and heard her voice from behind saying in jest, *"Do you always leave your women at sea?"* did he begin to consider that the fantastic had after all been true.

His amazement that she was suddenly there before him, looking glowingly beautiful and as if all the ailments that she had shown before were a thing of the past, stifled what he wanted to say. "You're not...I mean, you're okay...I thought..."

"I'm fine now," she said tenderly.

Yet Andale had many questions. "Did something happen to you before I found you? Were you attacked? Was it some sickness that took you?"

"I'd just been away from the water for too long, that's all."

"I don't understand."

"I'm here and I'm okay, but there are things I have to do now," she assured him with a gentle smile, before adding with a tinge of sadness in her voice. "I must go now, Andale, my gentle helper and everlasting friend. I'll not forget you."

"You know my name, but I don't know yours...or even where you come from."

"My name is Aoife, and I come from the sea."

"The sea?"

"Just the sea."

"You still seem troubled," he said then, his voice full with concern. "I'll walk with you to wherever it is you're going. I can help you do whatever you have to do."

Aoife's response was both resolute and volatile. "No! It's too dangerous, much too dangerous! No!" Then, when a consuming silence followed that left the sea-breeze moving between them as the only sound, she added softly, "Go home, Andale. It's not your business."

They parted then, the befuddled giant left alone on the dark shore while Aoife moved back inland where her lithe figure was enveloped by the darkness of the forest there. Yet the giant resolved quietly that her reluctance to allow him to accompany her was more out of concern for his wellbeing (and nobody had cared that much about him for such a long time) than it was for her own. Something happened to him too, when he stumbled across her weak bedraggled body earlier that night: it was as though he had found the something that had been lost. He knew too that the *something lost* was not Aoife herself, but the show of tender feelings that passed between them when he held her in his arms and looked into her eyes. After his parents died, he had lost himself in his wanderings. Every day there were new places to go and new roads to travel. There was no reason to care, and it was easy to lock away his feelings and to hide his true self. Yet the feeling that something was lost was a spectre that haunted his days and nights with a forlorn cry of want. Only when he found Aoife did that lonely cry cease and his true feelings return. Like reawakened and long lost memories, they all came flooding back to him when he took Aoife in his arms, and he knew then that he couldn't just let her walk away.

Instead, he gathered himself and, tracing the path that she would have followed through the dark forest with his eyes, began after her. Before long, he was close enough to hear her footfalls on the leaf-strewn forest floor and once or twice even glimpsed her moving through the trees not too far ahead. Yet he decided to keep his distance, stopping when he got too near to her and crouching down when she paused and turned as if to listen for a pursuer. When he finally left the forest, he lost his way and for a brief time became disorientated, not knowing what track to take, until he saw a shiny thread that had the same iridescence as that of Aoife's sea-dress, dangling on a tangled growth of nettles and this showed him the path to follow. When he caught up with her again, she was standing at the base of Linahen Rock looking up as if agitated. Her eyes were seeing something that he was unable to until he crept closer. In the shadow of a deep cleft at the bottom of Linahen Rock before where Aoife was standing, there stood a darkly clad man, a stranger who seemed to be blocking her way. A rush came over Andale as he watched them and his breath quickened when he thought that the stranger might be some dangerous attacker, but he held himself back for they seemed to be in conversation. For a moment, he thought that they might have even arranged to meet there and was considering turning away to continue his wanderings. The stranger could have been a friend of Aoife's, or a relative, or some other associate. Only when he saw Aoife trying to take the upward path and the stranger struggling with her before finally striking her down did he leap from his cover and go to her aid. Taken by surprise when Andale threw his great bulk down on him, the stranger tried to draw his staff but was unable to. After a most uncompromising struggle, the giant threw the stranger down with such force and determination that the stranger's body went limp and then fell silent. Already Aoife had made her way to the highest point of Linahen Rock, a sacred place, and had begun to sing a strange song with a lilting melody that spread like an infectious rain into the night. When Andale joined her, she was burning with ecstasy, her voice dipping with old cadences peculiar to Lissendel and then lifting with a wonderful piercing passion that was both unearthly and mystical. As if infused with a special knowledge, the bewildered giant was aware of the power of the amazing song and the changes it was already bringing down on Lissendel. Even in the depths of the night, there was a welling up of brightness that seemed to touch everything with such an exquisite radiance that it made the darkness dissipate before its time. It was a life giving canticle, a hymn to the former lushness of nature that invited its renewal, a call to the rivers and their spawning pools to flow again with fish and new life, to the fields to flourish and to be arable, and to the skies to turn with a normal cycle of the seasons that would bring a fair balance of days both clement and inclement.

When the song was finished and Aoife realized the help that once again Andale had freely given her and how she would have never succeeded in completing her quest without it, she reached out to him with an invitation to embrace. Although Andale was also a shy giant, he took no time in going to her, such was his captivation with the echoing remnants of her song that still filled the air all around, and the welcoming appeal of her demure beauty. They came together then in a heady second and held each other tenderly and silently, before sharing a brief, gentle kiss. There was no need for explanations between them and almost no need for words. They had been brought together, disparate islands adrift in a great sea, joined somehow by a progression of events and a track of destiny that neither controlled.

Garrett's eyes refocused on where he was then, because the story at that point came to a juncture where he felt that fact was interwoven with or lost in the realms of fantasy and conjecture. For what happened after to the female from the sea and the giant is still a subject of much debate amongst Lissendelians young and old. The fairies, the first ones to tell the story, happy that Lissendel's rivers were full with fish and that the land had been returned to its former lushness and that the weather was settled back into its natural cycle, returned to their underground hides and homes to celebrate, leaving the female and the giant at Linahen Rock bathing in the magical radiance of the renewal that both of them had created.

Varied stories followed after that: one that told of how the dark stranger, who was really a wizard of the black arts, had recovered consciousness following his tussle with Andale, and in a rage because of the astounding rejuvenation of Lissendel that was taking place before his eyes and that was thwarting his own insidious plans for its renewal, used his terrifying powers to bring the whole regeneration to a deathly halt. Demanding that an old decree attached to the *Song of the Salmon Girl* — that required that there should be the sacrifice of the life of someone associated with the song each time Aoife sang it — should be fully satisfied if it was to fulfil its promise, he left both Aoife and Andale stunned. He would have preferred Aoife to give up her life so that the song could never be sung again but was side-tracked by the giant who challenged him to a fight where the looser would offer his life as the sacrifice. And while Andale had great natural strength and was a man of unmitigated bravery, these were worthless against the black wizardry of the stranger who would not again be taken off guard by the giant's attack. In minutes only, the giant was stuck with temporary blindness by an immense flash from the wizard's staff and then, before he had had a chance to recover, entombed in a great chasm that he caused to open in a place on Linahen Rock where none had been before.

For a long time after that night the shadowy figure of the female would be seen drifting aimlessly out beyond the wash of the tides by the seashore. Sometimes, too, she would appear in dark forest lakes, fleetingly breaking the surface only to go under again and disappear. Other times she could be seen at Linahen Rock, her lithe ghostly form moving as silently as a feather as she cried for the giant Andale. Yet for all the times that the female from the sea had been seen, there had never been one sighting of the black wizard again following that night of the giant's death and Lissendel's renewal.

"I wonder?" said Garret as he ambled down the lane, quietly looking across the distance to that point in sky under which lay the approximate location of Linahen Rock.

CHAPTER 5

Maeve and Sammy were intently watching Garret as he strolled away in deep contemplation. They were both sure that he was working out a great plan that would see the fairies eventually releasing Sammy's sister, Dervla. And while Sammy was desperate to see his sister returned to their family safely, he was equally looking forward to again seeing a grand wizard such as Garret in action. He wasn't to know that Garret's steely determination and gift of magic powers would all too soon be put to the test and bent and tried to their fullest extremes. He was still lost in the anticipation of everything that could happen when an unnatural rumbling broke across what had been a clear blue sky, and then a black jinking shadow that appeared from nowhere came down onto the fields, where it began to grow and spread, before ominously moving towards where they were.

"Get back behind!" shouted Garret to Maeve and Sammy who seemed too frightened and dumbfounded to run away. For a frozen moment, they just stood still as suddenly the giant black shadow weaved from side to side with huge grasping feelers that proceeded, as it rampaged across the fields with ever increasing velocity, to suck in all sorts of everything and then spit them out in pieces. No sooner had the children begun to back away than a scream of fright went up and the hag broke over the hill and raced at full speed just ahead of a wayward grasping feeler of the immense shadow. As she made a beeline for where the others were, unaware that the main body of the monstrosity was gathering nearby there, she gasped frantically. "Help! Help! Somebody help me!"

Finally, Maeve drew back behind Garret. "What is it?"

Garret swung open his cape and pointed his staff upwards. "It's a darkness, some sort of shadow!"

"It's a monster!" wailed Sammy, as he started to run back to Garret, but he had only gone a short distance when he felt a tug at his right heel that caused him to trip and fall flat on his face. At first Sammy thought that it was the ravenous shadow that had snarled and tripped him, but when his right heel and then that whole leg was pulled backwards forcefully by what he recognized to be desperate grabbing hands, he knew that something else had snarled him. Instantly, he looked back up and saw that it was the hag who had entrapped him, her face contorted with terror as she grappled to resist her own entrapment from the pull and suction of another one of the shadow's advancing feelers. Sammy, too, could feel the pull and suction as he tried to push away, and it didn't help that the hag in her desperation was dragging him backwards into her nasty arms. Unwilling however, to give in, he kicked and pushed himself away but was released with a sudden ease that made him look again to see where the hag had gone. Just in time, he saw her being drawn backwards towards a raging orifice, her arms and legs flailing frantically and her eyes bulging with the effort of her resistance, but all to no avail. The shadow's mouth had come down on the road and with one great suck took her in and spat her out in pieces.

"Sammy! Sammy!" called Garret, but Sammy was unable to move such was his shock at having just witnessed what happened to the hag. Before him the shadow was coming together in the form of a gigantic floating fiend, its grasping feelers, eight in all, flanking out on both sides and turning inwards for attack, and its unsightly head that had only black holes in place of its eyes and mouth, coming down on the place where he was with a gaping snigger.

"I...I can't...can't move," he stammered desperately.

"Please, Sammy! Run! Run now!" cried Maeve.

Slowly Sammy lifted one foot, then the other, shivering with a growing trepidation that made him feel as if his legs were turning to jelly. As he backed away, the realization of the danger he was in was gathering in his mind with such panic that it made him fall over twice, but each time he picked himself up and continued his retreat. Before long, he found himself in full flight dashing across the open ground towards Garret as the shadow rounded in on him, its greedy feelers sucking from both sides and from behind. It seemed that the harder he tried to run the less progress he was making. In a flash, at the command of the rapacious shadow, two flanking feelers came round and down on either side, each with a cold sucking embrace that secured Sammy's arms and legs and pulled him back towards a desolate gaping hole at the centre of the beast that was its voracious salivating mouth. Garret moved swiftly too, waving his staff in a series of loops that sent huge fiery rings hurtling up into the sky where they lined up above the giant shadow.

"Impressive but useless!" said a voice that came from within the shadow, but its words had hardly been spoken when the fiery rings began to fall down to entwine its entire bulk and to rein in its floundering feelers. This caused the shadow to let out an unmerciful cry as it tried with all its strength to break free. "Ahhhhhhhhhhhhhhhhhhhhhhhhhhhhhhhhhhhhhhhhhhhhhh!"

"Let the lad go now, or worse will follow!" was Garret's unflinching response, as he pointed his staff directly at the centre of the shadow.

"I wouldn't do anything stupid if I was you," snarled the shadow, "not if you want your little friend back in one piece, as opposed to a thousand pieces."

"Who are you?"

"You might say that I'm a collector. Yes, a collector!"

"I see only a grotesque ghost, a shadow!"

"A shadow, yes! But look again! Look deeper! Am I not many? And is it not they you imprison with your cursed rings of fire? You can't hurt me without hurting them also, not to speak of your little friend."

There followed a series of tormented groans and moans by many voices from within the shadow. When Garret looked closer, he saw hundreds of shadows, all individually moving beneath the translucent skin of the great giant shadow, their figures and faces contorted and writhing in pain. This prompted him to ask aggressively. "What do you want?"

Both asking and answering its own question, the shadow seemed to mock Garret's question. "What does anybody ever want? More!"

"Let the boy go," retorted Garret, holding back the threat in his voice. "Surely he's of little substance to a giant such as you."

"Yes," agreed the shadow, indifferent and self-indulgent, "he's just a mere morsel to someone like me. But I've, you could say, my quota to reach and a hunger to pander to before I go back to the place from which I came."

"Which is where?" demanded Garret tersely.

"Hey, I've an idea," continued the shadow, ignoring Garret's demand. "We could do a trade. Yes, an exchange!"

Garret threw his eyes up resolutely. "I think I know where this is going, big fella."

"What a trophy a grand wizard such as you would make," laughed the shadow.

"So it's really me you've come for?"

"It won't be a painful separation, promise."

"What do you mean?"

"The boy for you, wizard," said the shadow impatiently. "Have we a deal?"

"I remember now," said Garret, his eyes distant with thought.

"You remember what, wizard?" queried the shadow, suspiciously.

"Are you not of the race of Mawlingfer from the region of Monn?" asked Garret.

Suddenly, the dark creature bulged with a mixture of malice and petulance. "Very good! But now Monn is at your door. We've come visiting abroad!"

"The Mawlingfer have always been peace loving creatures."

"Things change! You could say that we've woken from a sleep and now we need to harvest the crop that's before us. I'm just a forerunner of what's to come."

"What evil has come upon your race?" Garret asked, adding, "I can help you overcome it, whatever it is."

Almost instantaneously came a deathly cry from the Mawlingfer's inners, then the demands, "Enough of this! I'll let the boy go once you lay down your staff and step forward so that you and I can mingle."

"The girl must be allowed to go free, too."

"Agreed," retorted the Mawlingfer with painful groans, "but drop that infernal staff now and call off these fiery ring things!"

While the Mawlingfer's groans continued, Garret turned to Maeve and whispered with grave urgency in his voice. "Once he releases Sammy, run home to Creel as quickly as you can! This beast's not to be trusted!"

"But what about you, Garret?"

Garret's reply was as firm as it was concise. "Just do as I say and all will be okay!"

When Garret (much to the Mawlingfer's relief) used his staff to take away the fiery circles and then put it down, there was a moment when he considered retrieving it again and shooting fast at the beast, a ploy that he felt would have certainly thrown it into confusion and caused it to lose its grasp on Sammy, but he knew that if something went wrong that it would be the boy who would suffer most, and he couldn't take that chance. Instead, he edged away from where the staff lay and moved towards the Mawlingfer, saying: "I've kept my end of the bargain. Now let the boy go."

Instantly, Sammy found himself released. He seemed bemused at first and starry-eyed as he tried to orientate himself and to work out what was going on, but once he had and the imminent danger that Garret was placing himself in became apparent, a heady rush of dread seized him and he dashed towards the stoic wizard, shouting. "I'm free! I'm okay! Run now, Garret! Run!"

When Maeve saw Sammy and heard his shout, she also began shouting for Garret to run.

All too quickly, the Mawlingfer too realized what Sammy was saying and ominously increased its size and gathered itself as if to prepare for a chase, but Garret just stood his ground, ignoring the children's pleas with the answer. "A deal is a deal."

"How noble," quipped the Mawlingfer, as it reined in its wayward feelers and brought them to bear on Garret with gushing winds that sucked and spat and tussled at everything all around them as they began to draw him in.

"Garret said that we were to run back to Creel as fast as possible when you were released!" cried Maeve, desperately. "He said that he didn't trust the beast!"

"We can't leave him!" retorted Sammy, as he watched Garret standing up bravely before the beast and its darkness growing around him.

When the cavernous Mawlingfer finally engulfed Garret, there were lightning flashes and deafening rolls of thunder and then silence as the growing beast regurgitated and belched out a fiery froth. This was followed by many tormented moans and despairing shouts and pained cries that came from somewhere within the beast to reverberated out across the fields with a horrible deathly knell. From where Maeve and Sammy stood, it sounded as if the owner of a weakening voice, a lone soul, was staging a desperate struggle against an overwhelming opponent. In the black bulbous ball that was the Mawlingfer a tearing asunder was taking place. From somewhere inside the spewing beast, they could hear Garret crying out with terrifying pleas and chilling shouts that made them fear the worse and to realize just how helpless they were to do anything about it. "*No! No! No!*" came the cries again and again. Then all went quiet and the Mawlingfer's hairy feelers broke away to each side as it came down fully on the lane and paused for a moment as if to consider its options. In another moment it gathered its black bulk into one shapeless bubbling mass and took off slowly across the field, weaving menacingly along the same familiar path that brought it there until it was completely out of sight.

"Garret's gone forever!" sobbed Maeve. "Forever!"

"It's my fault," agreed Sammy. "Why couldn't I run faster...?"

"You ran as fast as you could," said a voice from behind that immediately the children recognized as Garret's.

"You're okay, Garret!" smiled Maeve with surprise.

"You're not...?" added Sammy, shaking his head in disbelief. "I mean, you escaped! You got away from that terrible beast without even a scratch!"

"Well, I wouldn't quite say that," answered Garret, as both Maeve and Sammy began to notice something strangely different about him. That neither of them could say exactly what was different about him made them enquire again and again if he was okay and quietly question (when Garret looked away) if he was not just another changeling sent to fool them.

"There's a healer in Creel if you're not yourself Garret," said Maeve.

"I'm afraid a healer would be of no use to me," smiled Garret. "My ailment is beyond what a healer can heal."

Still feeling that he was responsible for what happened, Sammy stuttered gingerly with concern. "And...and what's your ailment, Garret?"

"Nothing you need to be concerned about just now," responded Garret assuredly. "It shouldn't cause me too much distress in the near future, which is why we need to make haste in getting your sister Dervla back from the little ones."

"You'll still be able to help us then?"

"Of course! I'll be working on getting her back for you, on that you can rely. This very night I'll go to Linahen Rock!"

"To see the leprechaun?" Maeve remembered.

"That is," cautioned Garret, "if he's willing to show himself, and taken that he is a leprechaun and not some malign spirit intent on causing nastiness. He might even be, God forbid, the most malicious type of all the little ones, an Amadawn!"

"But sure, isn't an Amadawn," said Sammy dismissively, "just a joker and a fool?"

Without hesitation a severe warning broke across Garret's face. "Don't be fooled by the fool. The Amadawn's greatest talent is to appear as being harmless but take his hand as a friend or a foe and you'll become just like him – a mindless fool!"

Both Maeve and Sammy shuddered at the thought.

"I hope Dervla keeps clear of the Amadawn," gulped Maeve.

"Don't worry," answered Garret assuredly, "the little ones will keep her safe as long as they believe that she can sing the *Song of the Salmon Girl*. Not even King Lugh himself will be as well guarded as will Dervla."

Sammy was still concerned. "But what will happen when they find out that she can never sing the song?"

"The little ones don't give up easily. It's a weakness of theirs. They'll keep trying and trying. They'll exhaust every available minute, using every conceivable method to get her to sing the song."

"And then?"

Garret smiled then to ease the tension that he saw on the Sammy's face, saying as he began to walk away across the fields. "By then, we'll have her back! That's my plan! In the meantime, you two go back home to Creel. Tell them there that I won't let them down and that I'm already on my way to bring Dervla home!"

"Will you be a long time away, Garret?" asked Maeve.

"As long as it takes," came the reply.

As they both waved goodbye to Garret, Sammy whispered side-mouthed to Maeve, "I think Garret's in pain and that he's trying not to show it."

"I think so, too. Sure we even heard him crying out when the beast had hold of him."

"He going to need help, you know."

"I know, but what help could we give him?"

Sammy thought for a moment as he watched Garret getting further and further away. "We could be his secret eyes and ears. We could watch his back for him! He'll never know we're there!"

"But what about our families? If we're away for a long time, they'll be worried."

"We're going to get Dervla back. That's all that matters!"

"Garret said that he would be at Linahen Rock this very night. So will we! We'll go back to Creel but only to get some food and blankets."

"There's plenty at our house," offered Maeve.

"Okay, we'll go there," answered Sammy, adding as they started down the road to Creel, "but we can't tell anyone what we're doing. No one, not even our parents."

CHAPTER 6

That evening as Sammy and Maeve skirted furtively around the tall fields that lay on the outskirts of Creel, they appeared only as smoky silhouettes against the rusty haze of the falling twilight. So as to make double sure that they were not seen by either family or friends, they followed a wide path that circumnavigated the town and brought them around through its deserted back streets that were even emptier than they had anticipated. Yet Sammy had a shivering feeling of worry that, even though all the houses seemed empty and the streets deserted, made him imagine that they were all the time being watched and even followed. A creak in a shadowy hallway and the bounce of a kicked stone in a dark lane were all that he had to support his suspicions, but he couldn't shake off the feeling that someone unknown was there out of sight in the shadows, secretly watching and pursuing them. As they walked on, they could hear a single voice reverberating in the distance off the walls of the houses in Creel's main square. It seemed that a meeting was taking place there, and although they were too far away to hear the exact details of what was being said, they could still hear enough to discern that it was about the impending consequences of the lack of fish coming to Lissendel's rivers and shores and of the failing crops and the threat that these presented to the very livelihoods of everyone there. Every now and then, it seemed that a new speaker would take over, and this would cause a stir of voices from the crowd followed by a boisterous chorus of shouts and cheers.

As the stirring rally of speeches continued in the distance, they reached Maeve's house first. A warm and welcoming cottage, it had a garden full of overhanging trees that would have given the place a dappled beauty during daylight but just then, as they were slowly being drawn under the dimming evening, gave it a peculiar menacing shadowiness. Once she saw that there were no lights on inside the house, Maeve quietly indicated for Sammy to keep watch while she slipped through the garden and went around the side. Moments after, a light appeared in the front window of the house and then she opened the front door.

"Nobody's home," she explained, somewhat relieved. "You can come in now, if you want."

"I'll wait here," whispered Sammy cautiously listening as everything in the distance where the meeting was taking place suddenly went silent, and as again he heard a sound nearer that made him shudder. "Everyone must be at the meeting, but now I think it's over, and they'll be coming back, and..."

"And what?" asked Maeve, quickly perceiving his unease when he failed to finish what he was saying.

"Just hurry, that's all!" he ordered abruptly. "Get enough food for the two of us so that we can have a good supper. Oh, and something to drink. We'll go straight to Linahen Rock now."

"But do you not want to go to your house too?"

"No, there'll be too much explaining to do. And anyway, my mother probably wouldn't let me out again, especially if she knew where I was going. Best if we just go straight to Linahen Rock from here."

"We'll need food for four then!" said a voice from behind.

"And enough for us all to drink!" added another voice.

Instantly, Sammy jumped, startled and bemused, only to see Louise and Padraig emerging from under the trees, their faces broad with questioning smiles.

"It's only you two!" said Sammy, relieved.

"Who did you expect, the king of the fairies?" laughed Louise.

From the window of the cottage Maeve shook her head in relief. "I had a feeling we were being followed!"

"Why are we going to Linahen Rock?" asked Padraig.

As Sammy began to tell them all that had happened that afternoon and to explain to them the significance of Linahen Rock his mind began to focus more on the journey there. It wasn't as if

Linahen Rock was that far away, for there were only four fields, two hills, a valley, and a small wooded area to cross from there to where it lay, but with night closing in and its gush of darkness swallowing the land, it seemed a lot further. The thought of the coming darkness and the trek through it continued to make him feel apprehensive, but when Maeve emerged from the house with two sacks full of food and drink, he bucked himself up and without hesitation led the others down the road. Before long, the night was all around them turning the road that led away from Creel into a skulking black serpent that was leading them astray. Cast on the roadside in the moonlight, and just before where they started to cross the foot worn path through the fields into the darkening landscape, he saw the dumpy figure of his own shadow leading the three slight shadows of the others. This made him feel a terrible responsibility but gave him the determination not to let them down in any way. Still, for a moment, he found himself wishing that he were at home tucked up in his bed, before he thought more of this and scolded himself for being so selfish. He knew that the job in hand, like any job, would not get done if he had just lain at home in his bed.

After an hour or so of traipsing through the darkness, they left the path and crossed through some deeper grasses and then through a yawning cluster of tall black beech trees whose branches seemed to be reaching down as if to entrap them. With much trepidation, they went into the night's deepness, nervously cowering from time to time when sudden gusts of wind created peculiar whistling sounds and came around them with horrible tingling sensations that made each one of them feel that they were being drawn deeper into a great spider's web. In the deep colourless landscape, every shape was an ogre and every sound a scream of fright. At one point, they started to run backwards in panic when the wind pushed a huge branch across their path, and it came crashing down, shedding showers of leaves everywhere. For a stricken moment in the darkness, it was a monstrous attacker, until they came to their senses, and realized just what had happened and together laughed (if a little nervously) at their own foolishness. Slowly then, they began to appreciate that the wind was a good sign, because it meant that they were getting nearer to the sea, a fact that was confirmed a minute later when the wind wafted with the stench of the rotted wash that the tide had brought in. Sammy knew that the hills before him, Treefellwells Hills, were the last ones before the sweep down to the sea and that in the hollow there between the small woods by the shore and the mountain paths was the massive white boulder that was known as Linahen Rock. He had expected that Garret would have already been there with the leprechaun, but there was no sign of either of them, just some ghost-like swirls in a slow mist that was rising through the trees where the land sloped away to the sea.

As they made their way to an outcrop of rock on a nearby hill, Maeve stopped all of a sudden and then shushed the others as she listened across the night.

"What is it?" whispered Sammy.

"I thought I heard something, too," Louise added.

Padraig listened some more. "Someone's crying, I think."

From below then came the sounds of a struggle taking place, with pleading yelps and cries like those that a small animal would make when caught in a trap. This was followed by a voice that Sammy recognized as being Garret's, saying with much satisfaction, "Got yeh, little man!"

"Garret's caught the leprechaun!" exclaimed Sammy, looking out over the precipice. "A real leprechaun!"

When Maeve and Louise looked down, they saw Garret standing before the diminutive figure of a red-haired, red-faced man who was dressed in grey and green and gold. The little creature was frothing with anger while frantically waving his fists and struggling with all his might to get away, but Garret had him secured on some invisible hook off which he was unable to escape.

"Let's go down," suggested Padraig when he too looked down over the precipice to see what was happening.

"No!" answered Sammy, firmly. "Garret would be annoyed if he knew that we followed him here."

"Well at least let's get a bit nearer so we can hear what they're saying."

Sammy was reluctant to move from where they were at first, but when the others began to scramble down the side of the precipice without waiting for his agreement, he just shook his head resolutely and followed them. It was only when they reached a cup-shaped cleft in the hill and could go no further down that they finally stopped. From there, the view down was unhindered but still one that offered cover from the eyes of anyone looking up.

Below, Garret had found the stump of a rotted oak tree and was sitting down on it calmly filling his pipe as the leprechaun continued his struggle before him.

"I must be cursed, Mister!" moaned the leprechaun, dangling helplessly. "Cursed by banshees and lost souls! To be tricked by a cheap magician! To be caught in his infernal trap! I truly must be cursed, Mister!"

"I've been called a lot of things," laughed Garret, "but never a cheap magician!"

"Are you after my gold, Mister?"

Again Garret laughed. "Gold?"

"I knew it. Another treasure hunter come to take what's mine. Another avaricious, grabbing, tight-fisted big fella out to relieve us little ones of our hard earned—"

"Hard earned?" interrupted Garret sarcastically.

"I warn you, Mister," cried the leprechaun with exaggerated tears. "My gold will bring you nothing but sadness. That's all it's ever brought me – sadness and misery! Terrible, terrible sadness, Mister. I'll be glad to see the back of it and the terrible, terrible, terrible sadness and misery that it brings!"

Garret shook his head and drew on his pipe, saying, "But I don't want your gold."

The leprechaun's eyes lit up with sudden delight then, but he immediately tried to hide this. "You don't want my gold? Great! I mean ... you really don't want my gold, Mister? If you don't want my gold, big fella, what do you want?"

"My name's Garret Dimple."

"Garret Dimple, the w-wizard, the famous wizard? Of course, I knew it was you all the time, Mister. I mean, Mister Dimple."

"Call me Garret."

"Garret Dimple!" laughed the leprechaun. "As I say, I knew it was you all along. I knew that no cheap magician could conjure up such an ingenious trap as the one I find myself in. Speaking of which, do you think you could let me out of it now, hey Garret?"

"Oh I could let you go I suppose, but then you might just disappear and that wouldn't do, would it?"

"Me, Oliver Thaddeus Green, disappear? Never!"

"Oliver Thaddeus Green?"

"Everyone calls me Green."

"Well, Green, to answer your question as to what I want," said Garret, his eyes deep with sudden gravity. "I've heard stories, rumours if you like, about strange goings-on down underground in the kingdom old King Lugh. They say that he's captured the Salmon Girl. Know anything about it?"

"The eh-Salmon Girl?"

"Yes, the Salmon Girl."

"Eh...I know...eh, nothing about...eh, the Salmon Girl. Nothing."

At once Garret's voice became a threatening growl. "You're not a very good liar, are you, Oliver Thaddeus Green?"

Green's response was one of self-deprecation. "What can I tell you? I'm a mender of boots, a humble worker, and a not-so bright leprechaun. I'm a servant to those others who run around the countryside causing mischief. What would a little bundle of hard work such as I know about someone like King Lugh or the Salmon Girl and her song?"

Garret was quick to respond. "I don't remember saying anything about her song."

"Eh...sure," laughed Green nervously, "everyone's heard stories about her song, even me – not that I believe one of them!"

"What stories have you heard about her song then?"

Green said nothing for a moment but scratched his chin thoughtfully. "Well now, let me see…There was a story about… That's funny. I-I've forgotten how it goes. Anyway, there was another one about…No, I can't remember that either. There's one great story, a brilliant story, really, about the Salmon Girl, but eh…"

"You can't remember that either?"

"Don't know what's wrong with me. Maybe it's old age catching up with me."

"I'll tell you a story, you devious little imp!" snapped Garret sternly.

"Ah now," pleaded Green, "I'm to be pitied for my ignorance, not called names!"

"The story goes like this," continued Garret, his nostrils flaring as he rose and approached Green. "There was a devious and malevolent little imp, not unlike yourself, who took pride in holding back information about a certain young girl. The whereabouts of the girl was of particular interest to a very determined and some-might-say dangerous individual—"

"Who was, let me guess," interrupted Green sarcastically, "not unlike you?"

Garret ignored this. "The imp could have helped the girl by telling this individual where she was being kept, but chose not to. Instead, he lived only to serve the every whim of his own avaricious heart, which was like a great gluttonous stomach that each day required more and more food to satisfy it. Finally, the girl, only a child really, who was missing her family and friends and feeling so terribly lonely in a world outside of her own, lost her will to live and died. Her heart was broken, and her spirit crushed by things she never really understood! The imp's mind was never his own after he heard about her death. Although he tried to forget it, he never could. Not even his work would take his mind off what he should have done. The simple act of revealing where she was being held could have saved not only her life but also his own."

Green gulped with consternation at the thought of what was coming next but said nothing.

"Cursed by his own hardness of heart," Garret continued, "he could find no solace anywhere no matter where he went or in whatever he did. Even when he closed his eyes at night there was no respite, because sleep never came, just the ghostly image of a girl calling his name. So he took to wandering aimlessly each night on lonely roads and dark hills and lost fields in an effort to rid himself of the young girl's ghost, but it was all to no avail. The girl's ghost would haunt him for the rest of his days and there would be no escape from her pitiful cry! Each day would be a mirror image of the one before, and as his body slowed with age, it became as decrepit on the outside as it was on the inside. All because his greedy heart said no to what was right and good and caused the passing of a young innocent life from this world!"

"Right and good," repeated Green, feeling the full heaviness of the imp's troubles for a slow moment.

Garret eyes became cunningly tearful then. "Only then did he realize the terrible selfishness of his ways and came to regret what he had failed to do. But alas, it was too late! Too late to save the young girl and too late to stop his pathetic slide into a hell of his own making! Do you see yourself in all of this, Oliver Thaddeus Green?"

A panic shook Green until he stuttered uncontrollably. "I n-never wanted this, but...but—"

"You knew what was going on, didn't you?" interrupted Garret, a brutal demand in his voice.

Green became agitated for a moment, before his eyes displayed a remarkable sadness that was close to tears. "They'd banish me from this place if I told you where she was. I'm the keeper of Linahen Rock, you see. I'm not just another leprechaun as everyone thinks. Without this place, this place of secrets, I'm nothing!"

"Just tell me where the girl is. No one will know."

"King Lugh will take my gold!"

"I could take your gold," said Garret, raising his staff as his patience grew thin.

Green stuck his neck out resolutely. "You'll have to find it first! I'm not one of those lily-livered little ones who gives up his gold without a fight. Just let me out of this contraption, and I'll give you the fight of your life, big fella!"

"Then again, maybe if I took something else from you it would be of better benefit to me and worse to you!"

"Ha! Something else? But what?"

"Perhaps I'll take out your eyes so that you can no longer see the splendour of your gold," cautioned Garret playfully, "or will I cut off your ears so that you can no longer hear the jangle of its coins when you're counting them..."

"You're a cruel, cruel man, Garret Dimple," moaned Green with exaggerated distress in his voice, "to threaten to take away a little fella's only joy."

"It might serve me better though — now that I think of it — to take out your tongue so that you can never again call out *Phoulardnacrushnaparteenthomond!*"

Instantly, Green leapt up and fought the air with all his might to escape. "What? What? What? You know my word, my sacred word! You know my word!"

"I do," confirmed Garret. "Imagine never being able to utter it again!"

"Was it the whisperers who told you?"

"No. It doesn't matter how I came to know of your word only how I'll use it for my own gratification."

Above, the children were enthralled as they listened to the conversation. They grappled with each other to get a better view and a greater vantage point from which to hear and see what was going on below, but all the time were moving dangerously closer to edge of the slippery precipice.

Below they could hear Green shouting, "You don't want to mess with my sacred word, believe me!"

"Is it your word though? Did you make it up? What does it do?"

"It's my word, my word! And it's my business what it does, Mister, not yours!"

"But how will it do your business when you've no tongue left in your head to say it?"

"*Phoulardnacrushnaparteenthomond!*" exclaimed Garret at the top of his voice.

Green panicked. "Will you shut up or the whole of Lissendel will hear you!"

"But nothing happened," jested Garret. "Is it because I'm not up there on top of Linahen Rock? Let's go up there then!"

"No, no, no!" sobbed Green. "You don't know what you're doing, Mister! You'll ruin everything, everything, I tell you! How can I convince you?"

"Tell me where the king's holding the girl!" stirred Garret craftily.

Green shook his head with exhaust. "You're a hard man, Garret Dimple, a hard man indeed."

"Tell me where she is, and I'll not only forget about your word, but I'll set you free, too," said Garret moving closer to Green, as above the children crept nearer the edge of the precipice to listen.

Green was in tears. "It's up in the Great Northern Forest. King Lugh will have my neck for telling you this!"

"Tell me exactly where," demanded Garret. "The Great Northern Forest is a vast place with boundless places to hide such a slip of a girl."

"They're keeping her at, at—"

Green's voice was interrupted by a sudden sliding crash from above where Padraig, edging ever nearer the grainy ledge of the cliff face, slipped forward and in a desperate effort to regain his hold, which he just about managed to do, disturbed a small hill of stones that came tumbling down in a smoky rain. This brought Garret to his feet and caused him to draw his staff and point it upwards defensively, his eyes searching the skyline all the time for further activity.

Minutes went by in silence. The children crouched low and whispered to one another not to make a sound.

Sammy was quick to reprimand Padraig, with agitated whispers. "You eegit! Garret will be on to us now!"

"I slipped," explained Padraig.

Then Louise moved to look down. "They've stopped talking," she said, her eyes searching the darkness below, "and I can't even see them anymore."

"Did any of you hear where Green said they were keeping Dervla?" asked Maeve.

"No! How could we with all the noise?" snarled Sammy, glaring at Padraig.

Padraig cowered. "I'm sorry."

"Well, they're gone now," said Louise disappointedly.

"Tell me what to do next," asked Sammy with much frustration, "because I don't know?"

"I'm hungry," suggested Padraig gingerly. "We should have something to eat."

"There'll be no finding them now in the dark," complained Louise.

"Look, I'm sorry," admitted Padraig. "It's my fault we lost them."

Sammy realized then that he had only been trying to help. "Still, I think you had a good idea."

"What's that?" asked Padraig curiously.

"We should have something to eat before we go on!"

"Go on where?" enquired Louise.

"I heard Green saying something about the Great Northern Forest," said Sammy.

Louise's eyes deepened. "We're going back home to Creel first though?"

Sammy was in no mood to delay a moment longer than they had to. "In the dark? Let's just wait here till it gets bright. There'll be no time to go back to Creel though. It's the Great Northern Forest we're off to! Now let's eat some food and get the blankets out. There's a place back up the hill where we can settle down for the night."

Silent, each with their own reservations, they made their way back to the top of the precipice where the ground flattened out and a craggy overhang provided some rough natural shelter from the night. Maeve untied her sack there and opened it, taking out mineral water, home-baked bread, apples, and wheat biscuits, and distributing these amongst the others. Nearby, Sammy opened another sack and laid out four blankets evenly on the ground so that they all had somewhere to rest. They had only begun to eat when Maeve commented, "We've all heard of the Great Northern Forest, but has any one of us ever been there?"

All the others looked at one another with the sudden realization that not one of them had.

"I mean, how do we even get there?" she continued.

Silence fell on the others' faces like a heavy curtain covering an unforeseen dilemma that none of them had anticipated. It was only when Maeve innocently answered her own question that stifled laughter went up amongst them to allow a brief respite from their worries. "We could always pay Biddy-the-witch a visit," she suggested. "She knows where everywhere is!"

Padraig, grasping for a way out of a situation that he felt he had created when he slipped on the precipice and caused Garret and Green to flee, jumped with delight, "She's right! Biddy will tell us where to go!"

Louise had a question. "Does anybody know where Biddy lives?"

"I do," responded Sammy. "She has a house in the woods outside Creel. We'll go there first thing in the morning."

"Ok," Louise yawned jadedly in agreement, "but for now can we go to sleep, please?"

Despite the presence of what were to the children, strange and ominous sounds in the depths of the night, but that were really only a combination of those of the sea's wash coming ashore in the distance and the wind grinding the branches of the trees together in the nearby forest, they all found deep and undisturbed sleep until the sun's light slipped over the horizon to find them again.

CHAPTER 7

The next day Biddy was busy in her front garden, stirring a bubbling concoction in a huge black pot when the children came down the road. They stood there for a long time watching her apprehensively, each one of them afraid to ask what it was she was cooking. To them, it was a strange broth with a scent sweet and sour and unfamiliar and one that could only be known to witches and wizards. Indistinct amongst the trees, her house caused them to feel uncomfortable too, for it was rickety and dark, its windows all-seeing eyes and its doors laughing chasms that creaked open when the children got near.

Unaware that they were there, Biddy stirred the big pot adding powders and herbs as she hummed what to the children was a nonsensical melody, but still one that they found unusually enchanting. Even a gathering of black ravens in the trees above where they were seemed enthralled by Biddy's wordless song, as were some squirrels and hedgehogs and red deer and rabbits that had been passing by in the nearby woods but lingered just long enough for the children to glimpse them. Several times when the pot reddened and seemed as if it would boil over, Biddy snapped her fingers and released, to children's amazement, a sprinkling of golden dust that seemed to come from nowhere to cool down the broth again. Wandering closer as they fell deeper under the spell of Biddy's humming, the children finally came to her attention.

"Mouldy logs!" she exclaimed, for she had a habit of expressing her surprise with these words. "What are you all sneaking around here for? What do you want? Are you spying on poor old Biddy's brew?"

"No, no, no—" stuttered Sammy, shaking himself from the sleep that was about to take hold of him.

Impatiently, Biddy covered the broth and then taking Sammy by his collar, snarled threateningly, her eyes keen with questions. "You should know better than to come sneaking around here when I'm about my business!"

Sammy stuttered nervously. "W-we need...I mean, w-we thought..."

"We're on our way to the Great Northern Forest, Biddy," said Padraig boldly. "Can you help us get there? Or tell us which road to take?"

"The fairies are keeping Dervla there," added Louise, "in one of King Lugh's palaces."

"How do you know?" snapped Biddy suspiciously. "Who told you?"

"Garret Dimple went to meet Green, the leprechaun of Linahen Rock," Maeve explained. "It was the hag who told him that Green would know where they were keeping Dervla. And she was right. We followed Garret there and heard Green telling him that they were keeping her up in the Great Northern Forest."

Biddy's voice sprung with a question that had a warning. "Whereabouts in the Great Northern Forest? It's like a vast ocean with the darkest mountains and the deepest valleys and the tallest trees that have ever been seen. There are many dangers there and many pitfalls for the unwary traveller?"

Sammy spoke up then. "We-we don't know where exactly. Garret didn't know that we followed him to Linahen Rock. We were listening to what they were saying from a hill above where they were, but we made some noise just as Green was about to tell Garret where Dervla was being held, and it must have frightened them off."

"It was my fault," sulked Padraig.

The tone of Biddy's voice became threatening again. "So you were spying on Garret as well as me?"

"No, honestly, we weren't spying on either of you!" intervened Louise. "You have to believe us, Biddy."

"We were worried about Garret," Sammy said.

This made Biddy laugh. "Worried about Garret Dimple?"

Sammy took a deep breath. "Yesterday afternoon, we were attacked by a giant beast. Garret called it a Mawlingfer. It sucked up the hag and then took me. It was terrible! The hag is no more, Biddy. She was torn asunder by the monster! And I would have suffered the same fate, if Garret hadn't been so brave and offered himself into the arms of the beast in exchange for me."

Maeve took up the story then. "A great fight went on between Garret and the Mawlingfer then. The amount of shouting and crying was unbelievable. It was like there were a hundred different voices crying out in pain and desperation all at once. Garret was taken right in to the Mawlingfer's insides. We could hear him crying out with the pain. We thought he was done for. Really we did, Biddy. But he survived somehow. How, I don't know."

"There was something different about him though," interjected Sammy. "At first we thought he might be a changeling like the hag, but he was himself okay, just different somehow."

Again Maeve took up the story. "We asked if he was okay, and I told him that I knew a healer in Creel who could help him if he wasn't. But he said that his ailment was beyond what any healer could heal and that it shouldn't cause him too much distress in the near future but that it was important to get Dervla back as quickly as possible just in case it did."

"But all of you just can't go off journeying up to the Great Northern Forest," explained Biddy, concerned. "Have you told your parents what you're up to?"

"We're going to get Dervla back, Biddy," answered Sammy. "That's all that's important."

"We'll find where they're keeping her even if it takes forever!" Louise agreed.

"Nothing will stop us!" Padraig shouted.

"We're going to the Great Northern Forest with or without your help, Biddy," added Louise leadingly, "but of course, it would be better if you could show us the road to take."

"Garret needs our help, Biddy," pleaded Sammy. "I know he does. Something's wrong with him. Something terrible…"

After a while of walking to and fro Biddy softly mumbled the name *Garret Dimple* then retreated into her house where she remained for some minutes. This confused the children, for they weren't sure what she was thinking, even though individually they all felt that she would help them. When she finally returned to the garden, her two black cats, Penny and Pinch, followed her.

"Now let's see what we can see, my darlings," she said, going back over to the now simmering pot and uncovering it.

The children understood that she was referring to the cats when she said "my darlings" and not to them. This made Louise and Maeve giggle.

With her two cats purring and brushing lazily against her long black shawl, Biddy seemed to become unaware of the children again as she began to stir the broth once more. Long moments passed. Sammy was considering leaving, for it seemed to him that the morning was quickly approaching afternoon, and he feared that by the time night was upon them that they would still have made no progress. But as he rose to go, he caught Biddy's eye, and she turned towards him.

"Over here," she said, her face lit by a sudden remarkable radiance that came from the broth. "Come and see. Come and see my special brew."

One by one, the children approached the huge pot, again almost becoming enchanted when the old witch began humming once more. The unearthly glow that lit her face was soon on all of their faces, for there in the clear simmering swirls of the broth was a light that shone like no other and one that none of them had ever seen before. Within its magical brilliance, they all felt dumbfounded as a life-like picture began to form. It was as if they were moving down a winding path that was worn in some places and overgrown in others. It ran parallel to a rushing river and then away from it through a dappled part of a tall forest that was nestled in a tumbling green valley. There, the path sank out of sight only to become visible again some way further along where it cut through a lush plain and then snaked its way up to a moss covered wooden cottage that was sitting out on the spur of a yellow hill.

"It's amazing," enthused Sammy.

"Yes, but where is it?" asked Louise.

"It's a long distance from here. It's where Garret Dimple lives!" answered Biddy. "I asked a question of my special broth, and this is its answer."

"It's beautiful!" exclaimed Padraig.

"You'd think it was real," remarked Maeve.

"Oh, but it is real," replied Biddy.

Louise asked then. "What question did you ask it, Biddy?"

"I just asked where Garret Dimple was at this very moment."

Maeve frowned. "You think we should go there first, Biddy?"

"If you want to help Garret, you best let him know it," said Biddy wisely. "He'll want to look out for you and to protect you all. He won't be able to do that if you go sneaking after him without him knowing."

"Biddy's right," agreed Sammy. "It's best if he knows we're with him."

Louise wasn't convinced. "I know, but save he doesn't want us with him?"

Sammy voice fell glumly. "I just don't know what we'll do then."

"Garret's a fair man," Biddy told them. "If you show him the same steadfast determination to get Dervla back that you've shown me here today, he'll not deny you the trip."

"First of all tell us how to get to his house, Biddy?" asked Louise.

"Eh," hesitated Biddy, "having never been there myself before—"

"She doesn't know where it is!" interrupted Padraig.

In the moments that followed, Sammy thought about his home and about how nice it would be if Dervla were there and everything was returned to normal. Yet he could see no way that this would happen because it seemed that the harder they tried to come to terms with the predicament they found themselves in the more of a quagmire it presented. His head low with doubt and fighting back a dreadful sadness, he began to walk away, only to stop when Biddy's squeaky voice went up.

"You're right. I don't know where it is," she said. "Just that it's way north of here, near where an unnamed river runs between some mountains and the first woods of the Great Northern Forest."

"That could be anywhere," complained Louise.

"I might not be able to tell you exactly where it is," smiled Biddy towards her cats, "but my darlings will sniff out the way ahead for you and lead you to Garret's Dimple's very door."

Padraig coughed with disbelief. "Your cats?"

"Penny and Pinch, my special, special, special darlings," said Biddy, gently stroking the purring felines, "have senses beyond the ordinary. For them far away is no distance, and the darkness of night becomes as though it were daylight. They'll keep you on the right paths. They'll keep you away from the black regions."

Sammy gulped. "The black regions?"

"The black regions of the dark one who is really to blame for all our present misery."

"Is he the same evil one in the story about the giant Andale and Aoife, the Salmon Girl, at Linahen Rock?"

"Yes. Evil he is...to the core. They call him Largol. Largol Despalt is his full name. Not much is known about the Despalt family, but I wouldn't be surprised if they were in league with the devil himself! If we stray onto Largol's land — and it runs far and wide, mind you — we'll all be goners! Understand?'

"You said 'we,' Biddy. Does that mean you're coming with us?"

Biddy was genuinely worried about the children and the journey they were about to undertake but tried to hide this under the guise of concern for her cats. "Well, I can't let my darlings, Penny and Pinch, go wandering off into the woods with just anybody, now can I?"

"And where are these black regions?" enquired Padraig, his eyes wide with apprehension.

Biddy hunched down and with a twig drew two crosses on a patch of burnt ground next to her stove. "Between here and here and Garret Dimple's place," she explained gravely. "They're not on any map, and there are no true borders signifying where they begin and end, but we'll know we've crossed into the black regions, if we ever do by the deathly feelings that we'll experience of being followed and watched everywhere we go. There is a way around, but we must be careful because there are powerful snares laid on the outer reaches of the black regions with the sole purpose of drawing in all those who wish to pass by."

"Have Garret and Largol ever fought?"

"Garret and Largol are sworn enemies. No one knows which one of them is the more powerful. They've avoided each other for years because of this, but now it seems that Largol is itching for a showdown. If he had the right bait — perhaps one or all of us — to draw Garret into a fight, it might just suit him to do that now! That's why we must be cautious and careful. Cautious and careful, mind you!"

"Do you think that Largol already knows about Garret's fight with the Mawlingfer and how it's affected him?"

"I don't know. Perhaps Largol caused it to happen though. He's devious enough for anything, that one."

Sammy clasped his fist. "I just hope I'm there if they ever cross paths! What a fight that would be!'

Maeve was impatient. "When do we start for Garret's?"

Almost immediately a stern look flared up on the Biddy's face as her eyes searched those of the children with a grievous warning. "You might have to go without food! You might never see your loved ones again! You might be lost forever! Largol might get you all! Know this: nothing comes easy. Everything has a cost, and if you want Dervla back, you're going to have to pay a price. What that price is, only time will tell."

The children said nothing but glanced to one another anxiously as Biddy again walked to and fro with increasing menace in her eyes. "I ask all of you one question and one only." She continued, "Are you ready to sacrifice everything to bring Dervla home?"

Again the children glanced at one another, but this time they found a silent determination in each other's eyes that bound them together and gave them an answer. "Yes!" they cried. "Yes, we're ready!"

They had hardly uttered their answer when a sudden tremor ran through the ground beneath them, causing a tremendous shower of leaves to fall in the nearby woods and a desperate scampering amongst some little animals that had gathered in its undergrowth. Biddy's eyes grew stern with a mixture of fear and caution as she ushered the children to her side for cover. It was a sign, she thought, a bad omen, but she said nothing just then until she glanced a murky change coming over her bubbling broth.

"You've got no time," she whispered mysteriously.

"Was that thunder?" asked Sammy excitedly.

"It was no thunder," answered Biddy.

"It was like an eruption!" shouted Padraig.

"It was no thunder and no eruption! It was an omen!" she warned, with a mortal shriek as the murkiness in her broth began to spread and grow. "Be on your guard, young ones. My brew is speaking to us, showing us, warning us. Look how it changes!"

The children stood back with unease as they watched an ominous darkness clouding over Biddy's broth. The beautiful life-like picture of the winding path as it ran away from the rushing river and through the dappled part of the great forest that was nestled in the tumbling green valley, and then sank out of sight only to become visible again some way further along in a lush plain where it snaked its way up to Garret's moss covered wooden cottage that was sitting out on the spur of a yellow hill, was no more. All of a sudden, a shadow had slipped over it and engulfed its colour and light with an unrelenting cloak of gloom that boiled and belched with a foul-smelling stench.

Within an hour, their trek through the great forest had begun. Biddy spoke little before they left but busied herself during that time preparing food packs and blankets and oil lamps for their journey and then distributing these amongst the children to carry. Then she wrote a letter to Sammy's parents that explained where they were going and why and how long she anticipated it would take. It wasn't a long letter but one that gave them adequate information about the journey they were about to undertake, something which she hoped would put them at ease, while also giving them some small degree of expectation that their daughter Dervla would be home at the end of it. She included messages saying *not to worry* to the other children's parents, too, and entrusted Sammy's mother Marcella to pass these on to them with her assurance that they would all return home safely. For a while, the children were puzzled as to how she would deliver the letter for there was no postal service for those areas. Biddy, however, had her own tried and tested postal service that never failed, but when she stood up on a tree trunk with her arm raised and began cooing, Sammy and Padraig found this so amusing that they had to turn away to hide their laughter from her. However, they were soon wide-eyed with amazement when a fluffy white dove glided gracefully through the trees to land down on the perch that was Biddy's arm. With renewed respect they watched her rolling the letter in a scroll and gingerly tying it to the dove's leg while whispering something to it that they could not hear, but which they quietly agreed must have been Sammy's home address, before launching the delicate bird up into the air from her outstretched hands and then turning to join them for the journey.

For four hours, they trudged through the dense under-growth, Biddy and her cats striding out in front followed by the children who were all tiring as the deep tangle of trees closed in around them. The further they marched on the more they began to experience a feeling of being lost. Under the massive darkening canopy of twisted greenness, they were diminutive, and although Biddy seemed unaffected by how tiny they were against the great forest, the others felt as if they were slowly being devoured by it. It was only when the light began to fade and strange fluttering sounds came out from a dim clutter of trees nearby that even the old witch began to stumble and to lose her stride. Squinting into the darkness that lay ahead, her heart thumping, she stopped abruptly when she thought she saw a face.

"Children!" she said, as if to warn them (before then real-izing that it may just have been her imagination playing tricks) stuttering, "W-we c-could stay h-here tonight. As good a place as any...I suppose."

"I thought she'd never stop," complained Maeve jadedly.

Louise looked around as a last slant of light came through the hollow intertwine of wood that overhung and surrounded them. "Could she not have picked a darker place to stop?" she asked sarcastically.

"Least there's shelter here if it rains," said Biddy, as Sammy and Padraig began to unroll the blankets and light the oil lamps.

Padraig rubbed his hands together, saying, "Now for the food."

When they had all eaten and settled down, the great forest seemed a more hospitable place. In the glow of the lamplights, it seemed safer and warmer too, and yet several times after they had gone to sleep, Biddy jumped awake with breathless anticipation, sure that she had heard noises of hurried slashing and rustling coming nearer from out of the shadowy depths of the forest. However, it was not solely these noises that bothered her but the sudden stillness and silence that followed them. It was as if everything had stopped in waiting for what was to come. With her tiredness an increasing burden and knowing that she would need all the energy she could muster for the following day's journey, she quietly called Penny and Pinch to her side. The cats were at home in the darkness and could see through it, but still Biddy warned them about the strange noises she had heard earlier and about the face that she thought she had seen, before entrusting them to stay awake and to keep watch for the rest of the night and then finally going to sleep herself.

In the morning the children awoke with the sun warming them through a lifting silky mist that had come upon the great forest during the night. As it brightened, it seemed that everywhere around them was brimming with life such was the noise of the little creatures that lived there. Birds were singing, squirrels foraging, frogs croaking, and deer calling to one another. It was nature's bountiful music, performed by a fantastic orchestra made up of her small creatures as they went about their ways. As the children listened to it all, they heard another sound, distant but nearer. "Penny! Pinch! Where are you?" came the sound of Biddy's concerned voice, some way off through the trees.

"Her cats must have run off," said Padraig to Sammy.

Sammy said nothing. He was already busy opening the food packs to prepare breakfast. It wasn't that he was overly hungry either, but he suspected the others were, and anyway he just wanted to get breakfast over with and to get on with the journey.

Louise, realizing that Biddy was getting nearer, whispered, "There was something about those cats I didn't like."

"Me too," agreed Maeve.

"Penny and Pinch have disappeared!" complained Biddy, pushing through the trees. "I've searched high and low for them but they're nowhere to be found. They've vanished into thin air!"

"They've probably just gone home to your house, Biddy," suggested Sammy.

"They wouldn't just run off like that — not my darlings," replied the old witch.

"But sure, what could have happened to them?" asked Padraig to his instant regret when he saw the fierce look on Biddy's face as she swiftly turned towards him.

"Someone or something was out there in the forest last night...watching us," she croaked, eyeing the woods carefully. "I saw something."

"It was so dark here last night, Biddy," reasoned Sammy, "and you were tired. We all were—"

"You think it was my imagination?" interrupted Biddy, sternly. "Maybe it was and maybe it wasn't. Maybe there was someone or more than one waiting for the chance to pounce! Or maybe, as you say, I was tired, and it was my imagination. All I know is that Penny and Pinch, my precious darlings, are gone. Before, they would always come when I called, but not this time. Something's not right, I tell you!"

One by one, the children gulped with a growing sense of unease as they remembered the tangled darkness of the great forest the night before. Each one of them realized, too, that had they then been aware of Biddy's fears that they were being watched, even under the considerable weight of tiredness that they were all feeling because of the journey, they might have never found sleep. For Sammy, preparing breakfast had been a waste of time as all of them had suddenly lost their appetites. At least, he thought, there would be no further delay in them continuing the journey, but as they did, he noticed that not only had they lost their appetites but also, now, none of them were saying anything.

They climbed and walked for hours through the dappled forest, a resolute line of pilgrims searching for something that seemed impossible to find. The land rose and fell beneath them as they went on under a cover of trees split with sunlight where the smell of rot grew as the temperature rose. Some parts of the great forest seemed locked in a green mesh of darkness that even the sun couldn't penetrate, and it was when passing near to these blackened dens that they all found themselves moving closer together, as if some hidden voice had warned them that they should. Blindly, they followed Biddy's quickening lead under and over fallen trees and in and out of the overgrown rut. They stepped quickly behind her in a hurrying traipse that slowed only when they came upon some block in the natural path where a boulder or a leaning tree made it difficult for them to pass. And it was where one of these almost unscalable blocks, a massive moss-covered boulder, caused them to divert from the natural path that Biddy began to experience a feeling that all was not as it should be. She had travelled that path some time before and never remembered seeing the monstrosity there that was the boulder. With no rivers nearby to carry it there and no mountains from which it could have fallen, she thought, where had it come from? To the children, it was the head of an enormous fiend that had a slimy green face with black hollows for eyes and a sneering gash for a mouth. No longer did Biddy feel in control of the direction they were taking because the diversion was leading them around and away from where she had intended to go. She quickly realized, too, that the more she tried to return to her original path the more it seemed to have disappeared. The forest had become a consuming maze of trees that hemmed them in on three sides and closed behind them as they went forward.

CHAPTER 8

Hour after hour, they followed the unknown track that the forest presented. At mid-morning they finally emerged on the crest of a jagged hilltop where a last line of pine trees fell away to a sunlit clearing. Below there, and sweeping down and up again like the bowl of a vast amphitheatre, a meadow full of gigantic flowers of every colour and shape stretched out before them, providing a gaping divide between one side of the great forest and the other. Beyond this were the blue and grey peaks of the Winterlan Mountains and further off to one side another fall of land that led down to a black beachfront that was bordered by the slim teasing whitewash of a velvet sea.

Louise gasped with exhilaration in the warm breeze that lifted across the open land. "Look! We're on the roof of the whole world!"

"I've never seen so many flowers," added Maeve. "Look at all the colours! And the size of them!"

Sammy was worried. "Where are we?"

"It can't be the black regions anyway...can it?" Louise asked.

"We're lost, if you ask me," cautioned Padraig. "But it looks like a good place to have a rest and something to eat."

"Good idea," agreed Sammy, now hungry for the breakfast he missed earlier.

Biddy said nothing but pulled a strange face as she sniffed the air and scanned the whole landscape. Then, before she sat down with the children, she lifted a finger into the breeze and then sniffed it, saying: "Eat quickly! We'll have to find some shelter. Because unless I'm mistaken, there's a storm on the way."

Again Sammy felt his appetite drop away, but this time he forced himself to eat because he knew he would need to keep his strength up for all the trials that he suspected lay ahead.

Biddy's prediction that a storm was coming was something he dismissed however. Although he knew she had special powers as a witch that would allow her to sense things before they occurred, he found himself doubting that she had correctly predicted the storm because up until then the day had been warm, sunny, and pleasant. However, barely had they finished eating than he noticed a change coming over the skies with the blue brilliance that had been there from early that day giving way to a huge bank of tormented grey clouds that came and sat over both sides of the great forest, unpromisingly. Even then, it failed to rain but slowly got darker and darker until the magnificent colours of all the giant flowers in the meadow became nothing more than different shades of the same angry greyness that had invaded the skies above them.

When the rain finally came, it was a roaring torrent that seemed to be released with greater vigour at each clash of thunder and snap of lightning. A roaring wind rose too, taking Biddy's breath away when she shouted to the children to make for the shelter below in the meadow that was provided beneath the canopy of the then closed blossoms of the giant flowers.

"Let's go!" roared Sammy, leading the way down into the thrashing meadow of flowers.

The others followed him down the slope without delay, moving slowly at first until the weight of their bodies and the steepness of the incline combined to thrust them all down at a faster rate than any of them had been prepared for. Padraig, always moving faster than the others, was quick to reach where Sammy was but lost complete control of his movement and tumbled down to take him with him over a greasy ledge. The two rolled and tumbled and slipped in a murky mudslide and only came to rest in a muddy pool where the meadow flattened out and the giant flowers stood. Louise and Maeve, when they arrived down the slope, couldn't help laughing when they saw that the only parts of Padraig and Sammy that were visible beneath the mud that covered them were the whites of their eyes and teeth. Biddy, however, was more concerned with their new surroundings, for never before had she seen such monstrous flowers, and although the storm seemed less of a threat under the great canopy that they provided, she was unable to rid herself of the feeling of somehow being captive.

The children, on the other hand, were quick to find a comfortable place where they could shelter until the storm blew over. It was near the centre of the meadow between the tall arching stems of a bunch of daffodils and a raised walk of tulips. Not only were they sheltered from the raging storm by the gargantuan flowers, but they were also provided with water to drink and (to Padraig's and Sammy's delight) to wash with, from pools where the rain had been channelled off to the sides and had gathered in huge fallen petals. While the muddy boys washed, Louise and Maeve collected some dry twigs and grasses to build a fire. Biddy, seeing how quickly the afternoon light was fading, was more suspicious than ever about the whole place. She could not content herself for them to stay there for the whole night but knew that they had no other option. They were at the mercy of the storm, and its ferocity was dictating that they should go no further. But what was it, she thought, that was making her feel so uncomfortable? Was it the unusual size of the flowers? Was it their vast amount and exotic nature? Was it the fact that most of them were alien to that place, and that some were even out of season? *No, no, no!* she whispered internally, and then looking skywards almost found an answer when she had a shivering sensation of being watched.

When the storm finally died, the meadow was overtaken by the purple cover of night. In the vast stomach of darkness that the forest of flowers had become, the only light was that of the dancing flames from the small fire that Maeve and Louise had started. It was that light too, that gave them hope and more than they knew, for it was keeping them safe from the clutches of the terrible entanglements that were lurking all around. However, they were unaware of these dangers and unaware of how treacherous their very silence was to their wellbeing just then, yet strangely none of them were feeling talkative. The long haul through the great forest, the storm, the night and the warm glow from the fire had all combined with the silence to make every single one of them just want to sleep. And it was when they all had and the fire began to die that the creeping around and towards them began.

Biddy's sleep was burdened by a fiendish spectre of doom. In a tear away nightmare that had no way out and no ending, just a slow terrible continuance, she cowered before hideous pursuers and fought to escape their sticky entanglements. But when she tried to run, her feet carried her nowhere, and when she screamed, there was no sound. Everything everywhere was reaching after her, as if to ensnare and to trap her. Beast things came from above and below with black slimy tentacles that gripped and pulled and squeezed and throttled. And although she refused to give in and struggled and fought for all she was worth, with such great odds against her, she felt herself slowly beginning to weaken. It seemed that she was alone against an army of uncompromising foes and that they were unrelenting in their pursuit of her and always gaining ground. Yet she fought on, pushing them back with desperate lunges and frightening threats, only to find more attackers coming from a darkness behind and below to drag her back and down. The struggle went on in her sleep, while her arms flailed about for real as if it there was an actual struggle going on. Only the children could have said if her struggle was real or not, but they were also asleep. They were not to know how soon the black slimy tentacles that gripped and pulled and squeezed and throttled would invade their dreams also, to drag them down and under.

All would have surely been lost if it had not been for the cat cries and meows that came not a second too soon to awaken Biddy and to warn her that the wretched ghosts that troubled her nightmare were not those of a disturbing dream but ones very much alive and real.

"Penny! Pinch! You've come back!" shouted Biddy, while slowly becoming aware of the stealthy movement above and in the undergrowth around them.

At this moment, all the children woke. No sooner had they become aware that Biddy's cats were back when they saw the fear in their eyes and then realized that their comfortable place of rest was beginning to move. Above, the giant flowers were bending over and coming down, their blossoms like grotesque heads with mouths full of jagged teeth that were opening and closing, while below the slimy black tentacles of their roots were reaching out from under the ground and snaking towards them ominously.

"Mouldy logs!" shouted Biddy, jumping back and gathering the children and her cats around her as the giant flowers and their roots began to close in around them.

"What'll we do?" shrieked Louise. "I think they want to eat us!"

Maeve sprung up in panic. "Run! Let's run now before it's too late!"

"No," answered Biddy, who had become aware just then of how the giant flowers and their roots were avoiding the place where the fire was even though it was no more than just a heap of smouldering dust and dying embers.

Already, Padraig was backing away. "What will we do then? They're almost on us?"

"Look how they avoid the fire!"

"We'll do this then," said Sammy boldly jumping out and taking a half smouldering twig from the fire and swinging it wildly at the monstrous flowers and their roots.

A minute after, Biddy and the others were also swinging half burned twigs that they had taken from the dying fire. Slowly and reluctantly, the giant flowers and slimy roots gave way, moving back to where they came from.

"It's working," agreed Padraig, with some relief. "They're backing off."

In all the excitement not one of them noticed that the fire had now died completely. It was when the twigs that they had armed themselves with began to burn out and they went back to the fire to replace them that they discovered that it was no more.

"Quick," called Sammy, rushing to where the fire had been and blowing on its dead embers in an effort to revive it. "We can't let the fire go out!"

The others rushed forward then, gathering any dry twigs and pieces of wood that they could find and placing these down on the lifeless fire. Then, with a combined effort of much blowing and puffing, they nursed life back into the dead embers, until finally, smoke billowed upwards and a red glow came under them and the fire rose again.

"We've done it!" cheered Maeve breathlessly.

"One of us will have to keep watch over it all night to make sure it doesn't go out again," said Louise.

Suddenly, a great shaking disturbance came from above and around them. None of them understood what was happening at first, until Sammy looked up and saw, to his shock, the giant flowers swaying from side to side to release the murky deluge of rainwater that had gathered in their canopies. He never even had the chance to warn the others before the filthy rain came down to soak all of them and to fully extinguish the fire.

"We're helpless now," he whimpered to the others when a creaking movement replaced the shaking disturbance as once again the great bulks of the giant flowers and their slimy black roots began to close in on them.

With no possible escape in sight, they all huddled together in complete darkness as bit by bit the monstrous plants surrounded them in an ever-tightening circle. They had all but accepted that they would be snapped up and eaten there and then, when, at the very moment that the huge salivating blossoms were gaping open over them and about to snatch them up and just as their slimy black roots were about to entangle them and drag them under, a flash went up and shot right through the heart of the tallest of the massive flowers, stunning it to its roots.

Through the darkness they saw a shining light, a sword perhaps. Frantically, they broke from their huddle with new hope as the severing light thrashed through the enormous stalks of the giant flowers, cleaving off their screaming blossoms and cutting them sideways and down. With a whirlwind of chops and slashes, the light cleared a path to them and then sliced a greater space around where they had been trapped. Moving at great speed, it rasped the sides of all the giant flowers that were nearby so that they moved far back and then even cleared a path to the far end of the meadow.

Just then an orange sun rose over the mountains and crept along the path that had been cleared until it reached the feet of Garret Dimple who stood there with his staff shining still as it had been when he used it like a sword.

"Mouldy logs!" exclaimed Biddy in wonderment. "Garret, it's you!"

The children danced with delight. "We're saved! We're saved!"

Briefly, Biddy danced with them. In her jubilation, she almost forgot to thank Garret for saving them but then remembered and broke from the dance to take his hand. "You've done a great deed, Garret Dimple, this day. You're truly blessed, you know. We would have all been lost without you."

"Thank these two," smiled Garret, stooping down to pat Biddy's cats, Penny and Pinch. "They came to my place and made me follow them here."

"My precious darlings!" repeated Biddy again and again, taking both cats up into to her arms and hugging them lavishly.

"We-we better go now," coughed Garret then, a weakness in his voice.

Cautiously, Biddy put her cats down and turned to Garret. "Are you okay?"

"Yes, yes, but we should go now to my place. Quickly!"

"Yes. Okay," responded Biddy concernedly, as the children too became aware of Garret's weakening condition. And when moments after he collapsed, mumbling again and again that they must go and go now, they began to fear that there would be another onslaught of the giant flowers and their roots and that this time there would be nobody to rescue them.

"They're coming back for us!" warned Louise, watching the monstrous flowers regrouping.

Propping Garret up and giving him his staff for support, Biddy growled to the others who were all trembling with fear as they watched the flowers starting towards them. "Help me to get him to his feet! We've no time to lose."

"Don't fuss, woman. I'm okay!" snapped Garret as he struggled to his feet.

Biddy continued to help him up. "Maybe you should rest awhile…"

"I said I'm okay! I'll rest at my place and not before!"

"But you don't look yourself, Garret. You look sickly, weak—"

"Watch how I cut the plants and snap their husks when they come back at us," boasted Garret fearlessly, moving Biddy aside as he stood up again. "I'll show you who's sickly and weak!"

"What's happening to him?" Sammy asked Biddy.

"I don't know. But let's just get away from this godforsaken place now!"

While Biddy was still speaking, an early mist lifted to let sunlight with a greater resplendence than before spread over the entire meadow of the giant flowers, bringing down on them a deathly stillness that at first only Sammy, to his utter relief, recognized. Somewhere, he noticed too, that an early bird had begun to sing, then another and another and another. Before long, came the sounds of other animals moving through the undergrowth and foraging for food and calling to one another and dashing to and fro, until the meadow seemed alive with every sound and activity of nature except those of the giant flowers who were wilting and falling in on one another.

"Everything will be okay now," he said, walking a short distance away, his eyes brimming with new hope. "I think the giant flowers have gone to sleep or something."

Briefly, Padraig watched Sammy's marvelling at the chorus of birds and the fearless movement of all the small creatures through the meadow of the giant flowers before he placed a friendly hand on his shoulder to let him know that it was time for them to leave. When finally they turned to go, they saw Garrett hobbling away quickly, if a little unsteadily, to lead them through the clearing to the far end of the meadow. Even though they had to run to catch up with him and then walk quickly to keep up with the pace he was setting, they both saw a weakness in him that had not been there before. Was it the something that he had lost in his fight with the Mawlingfer that was now taking its toll on him? Although he still presented one solid and daunting presence and had performed a relative miracle when he rescued them from the grasps of the giant flowers, something about him that had been there before was definitely missing, and they began to fear that with the passing of time the lack of its influence would be felt more increasingly.

Chapter 9

It was night when they finally returned to the worn path through the great forest. Garret was still leading the way and seemed as surefooted in the darkness as he had been in daylight. After climbing steadily for hours, they reached a ridge where broken boulders and hills of shale stood out to scar the land. In silence, they scrambled down the winding slopes before negotiating the descent of a long sinuous crevasse that gave way to an even larger one and a sheer drop to the overgrown banks of a rushing river. The moon had risen high and was lighting a way for them by the time they found a safe place to cross. All was silent but for the sound of the river's whirling currents and the solitary whistling of a last bird flying late to its nest. Just a subtle breeze was all there was to temper the balmy air that rose from the forest floor that was itself adrift with the scent of decay. On the other side of the river, it was much darker, with undulating terrain and overhanging boulders that seemed to almost swallow the path that they were on and to totally negate the guiding light of the moon. Had it not been for the stolid and fearless way by which Garret was leading them, his cape flapping with an energy that was seemingly all its own, they would surely all have been lost. For there in the darkness of the overhang they were formless, just shadows lost against a greater shadow.

When the moonlight found them again they were in the last stretches of the great forest where it thinned out and sank into the obscurity of a tumbling valley. This place was suddenly familiar to Sammy. Beyond this, he remembered, if the life-like picture in Biddy's magic broth was accurate, there was a lush open plain and the spur of the hill (that would have been yellow in daylight) where Garret Dimple's cottage sat. The thought that they were so near to the cottage gave him comfort, but he still wished that they could get there quicker. He knew by the looks on the jaded faces of all the others that they would not be able to continue on much further. He had to remind Maeve and Louise about the life-like picture in Biddy's magic broth too, when they complained of being tired and hungry, to make them realize just how near they were to Garret's cottage and its comforts. The girls responded instantly with new vigour and vitality and went from trailing behind the group to joining Garret in leading it. This made Sammy laugh for a moment, but soon his thoughts turned to the questions that had been playing on his mind ever since they left Biddy's house. Would he really ever see his sister again? Would his family ever be complete and happy the way it had been before? For a strayed second his thoughts focused on the memories he had of Dervla, and in the depths of his mind he saw her face. *Dervla,* he thought, *I miss you. We all miss you. It's not your fault that you have a voice that makes the angels jealous. No wonder the fairies took you. I'm sorry for all the times I gave out to you. You're not bad as sisters go, and if we get you back, I'll never give out to you again, I promise. If I could just see you now for a second, I mean, really see you, it would be great. No, on second thoughts, a second would never be enough.* All at once Sammy's memories pierced through him with a wretchedness that was laced with doubts, but he knew that he had to keep strong and to show no weakness in front of the others. A new worry had begun to badger his thoughts and to trouble his mind also. Would any of them see home again? He was beginning to doubt that they ever would when a sudden shout went up from ahead that instantly uplifted his spirits and made him forget his wretched doubts.

"See how the lights grow brighter as we draw nearer!" came the cry from Garret, his voice both relieved and thankful.

"It's Garret's place. Thank heavens!" crooned Biddy, skipping onwards with Penny and Pinch.

Maeve and Louise danced for joy. "We've made it! We've made it!"

Sammy and Padraig just smiled at one another when they emerged from the darkness of the tumbling valley to the lush open plain that was bathed in the rustic glow of the welcoming lights of Garret's cottage.

It was indeed a warm and hospitable sight, and more so than any of the children had expected. Even Biddy found herself drawn in awe to the cottage's glow. For a moment, she was struck dumb and left open-mouthed with wonder when she saw the red and orange and yellow pulses of light glowing stronger as they got nearer to it. It was truly a magical place, she thought, and yet, although shining in its own strange and magnificent way in the darkness, it was the sense of its comforting homeliness, even before she entered it, that touched her most. It was as if the old cottage itself had been expecting them. Had it been anyone other than Garret's home, she would have questioned how such old quarters could have been so welcoming: its lights lit, its front door opened wide, its living room set with places for all of them, and its tables overflowing with all sorts of exotic dishes and broths. Biddy though, used to a whole world of strange happenings and unusual goings-on, knew never to question such good fortune and especially when it was connected to Garret Dimple. She was first to sit at the table and had begun to eat, much to Garret's amusement, even though the others were there before her. It was only after much meowing by her cats, Penny and Pinch, that she spared some meat from the table for them to eat and then emptied a pitcher of milk into a good-sized bowl for them to drink.

"Sit where you want, and eat what you can!" offered Garret, seeing a hesitance in some of the children.

Sammy and Padraig pushed forward then and sat at the table, followed by Louise and Maeve who were both so hungry that they simultaneously managed to catch a knocked-over tray of sandwiches before it hit the floor without dropping even one. This brought applause and shouts of "Well done!" and "Great catch!" from the others. It was just then that Biddy noticed a twinkle in Garret's eye, which suggested that he had somehow aided the two girls in catching the sandwich tray with the slight and timely use of his magic. Realizing that Biddy was on to him, he took a seat at the head of the table and with a raised eyebrow to her to acknowledge his *couldn't-help-it* involvement, laughed heartily saying, "Let's eat!"

Without any further hesitation they all drank and ate everything that had been laid before them. For an hour or more, it was as though they had forgotten all their troubles, past and present. Only Garret Dimple's memory remained fully intact. He knew that the warmness and the enchantment of the cottage would make them forget and give them, if only for a short time, some much-needed rest and respite that would help prepare them for what lay ahead.

Later that night with their stomachs full and their thirsts quenched, they moved round the heart of a huge open log fire that was located at the other end of the room. The children were all feeling tired but were also too excited to go to sleep, for there was a great sense of anticipation in the air. For some moments, Biddy and Garret whispered, and then the wizard stood and drew out a golden flute.

"Looks like we're going to have some music," said Louise to Maeve.

"Not just any music," Biddy added.

The moment Garret began to play, Maeve stood with fright. "It's the same tune they played at the fairy rath when Dervla was taken!"

"You sure?" asked Sammy.

"It's the devil's own music, I'm telling you!"

"Shush," ordered Biddy. "It's called *The Song of the Salmon Girl,* and it's not of the devil. Far from it."

As Garret continued playing, the glow from the fire began to intensify. Biddy and the children however, hardly noticed this. They were too captivated by the music that had suddenly made everything else seem of no consequence. All of a sudden a greater light began to show on all their faces as they reflected the warm orange glow of the fire's flames that swirled and pulsated and rose. The fire, constantly changing, crackled as it sent off tiny sparks of different colours in all directions before the flames themselves began to change to a wonderful dancing array of colour that had the same range and tones as that of a rainbow.

Then a great shining light, but not a blinding one, came from the fire and opened out around them. Within it, a shimmering face began to develop. It was a girl's face, *the Salmon Girl*, thought Biddy squinting, while all the children only saw the face of Sammy's sister, Dervla. Garret, however, saw both faces as if they were becoming one.

'Dervla! It's Dervla!' shouted Sammy, rising when the image in the fire reached out to him.

"Stay back!" warned Biddy, moving to stop Sammy going into the fire.

Garret, his eyes closed then, played on. His music was now a visible smoke, silvery-blue in colour, which encircled the whole room with a glowing bracelet of light that rose out through the roof of the cottage and across the dark stretches of the night.

All the time, Sammy was advancing on the fire, his face aglow. Through his eyes he saw no fire, just his sister, Dervla, reaching out to him.

"He's touched," remarked Louise.

"Sammy, stop! You'll get burned!" cried Padraig.

Instantly, Louise ran out in front of Sammy and shouted, "Stop Sammy, or I'll...I'll...slap you!' And it was only after she had slapped his face with all the strength that she could afford that she realized that she had done it before she had even got the words out.

Confused, Sammy shrieked and rubbed his face as the pain of the slap jolted him back to reality. "Ouch! What's ...?—"

"I'm sorry, Sammy," said Louise, shrinking politely with a half-smile. "I didn't mean to hit you that hard."

At the same time a black smoke billowed from the fire and began to engulf all the warm brightness of the flames and magnificent colours that had been there. Before the flames died completely, Sammy caught one last glimpse of his sister Dervla, her arms still reaching towards him, before a shadow came over her and took her away.

The music rounded off in a final lonesome pitch, a singular wailing cry that rose and then died as if drawing back all the sound that it had dispatched out through the night into one solitary note. Garret Dimple looked up then.

Biddy pondered dolefully. "So simple...and yet so powerful."

"Yes..." agreed Garret, lighting his pipe.

"If only I could sing it."

"It's the same tune the fairies played when they took Dervla," complained Maeve.

Garret said nothing for a moment. It was as if he needed time to think and yet his wizen features and bright eyes suggested that his thoughts came as fast as light. After one quiet puff of his pipe, he called everyone closer as if he was going to tell them a tale. The children were still talking excitedly after experiencing the magic music and the wonderful fire, but quietly he hushed them and then began to talk.

"You shouldn't have followed me to Linahen Rock the way you did," he said sternly. "My little friend Green became very agitated."

"Green, the leprechaun?" spoke Sammy. "We didn't mean to frighten him."

"And you were wrong to think that you should come gallivanting up through this neck of the woods," continued Garret, before he paused to stir his pipe and to tap it on the table.

"Yes, but we just want to get my sister back!"

"And you don't trust me to do that?" sighed the wizard.

"We do, but—"

"It's my fault for bringing them," confessed Biddy, winking to the children. "They were worried about you, Garret, and the state of your health after your run-in with the, what-did-you-call-it, Sammy, Mawlingfer?"

Garret said nothing for a long time but lit his pipe again and puffed on it thoughtfully. "My health is my own affair, witch," he answered finally, while ruefully eyeing Sammy, "and if I thought that the whole countryside was debating on whether I was on my last legs or not, I might have just given a deaf ear to your cats when they came crying for me to rescue you last night!"

"No one else knows that you're s-sick," stuttered Sammy. "I mean, that you're not your usual self."

"Sick? Not my usual self? Is that what you've been tellin' the whole countryside?"

"We didn't tell anyone. Honest, Garret."

Garret's face turned ashen with thought. "Are you sure? In these parts the trees have ears and the grasses listen for secrets. Many a life has been lost by quiet words spoken under oaks and willows and ashes and beeches. And many a soul destroyed by stories told by loose lips in those fields where the grasses whisper. So are you sure, young fella? Are you quite sure?"

Sammy gulped. "No..."

"The boy just wants his sister back," said Biddy, who knew by the way Garret was reacting that something about him was definitely amiss.

Louise, Maeve, and Padraig nodded to one another and spoke as one. "We all want her back!"

"Where is Green, the leprechaun? Did he run away from you?" Sammy asked.

Garret smiled to ease the tension. "He's probably back at Linahen Rock by now, the little moaner. I let him go...but not before he told me where they're keeping your sister, Dervla."

"So you know where she is?"

"It's still a good distance from here, and the roads that lead there are dangerous. I would have already been on my way there had I not gone back for you lot."

"We're all grateful you did, Garret," agreed Biddy craftily. "But what now? Are you going to leave us here or take us with you?"

Garret thought for a second. "As I said, *in these parts the trees have ears and even the grasses whisper secrets.* And because we don't know who might now know of my run-in with the Mawlingfer and what it's done to me, I think it would be best if you were not to remain here. Because even here, there would be a danger that one or all of you could be taken and used to bargain me away from what I have to do."

"And we could suffer the same fate, if we tried to go back to Creel."

"So it looks as though, and it's against my better judgment, mind you, that I have no option but to take you with me."

Sammy jumped up. "We should go now then!"

"It's been a long day, and we all need to get some sleep," answered Garret, seeing the tiredness on the faces of Biddy and the others.

"But we—" protested Sammy, only to be interrupted by the wizard.

"Tomorrow!" He said, smiling sternly. "Tonight we rest."

CHAPTER 10

That night, Sammy found it difficult to sleep at first, but was relieved that all the others had. His mind was continuously grinding over all the things that had happened since his sister had been taken, and he was still troubled by self-reproach, feeling that his efforts to stop it happening had been inadequate. Yet before long, even his racing mind began to slow beneath the gently swaying eaves of the rambling cottage, and he found himself drifting towards sleep but still never finding it. Even though they were all bunched cosily together in what Garret called *the small upper room*, a truly restful place, sleep evaded him. That the room had been prepared in advance for them with five makeshift beds and a cosy fire kept him from fully falling to sleep too, such was his sense of awe at the magic that Garret, who had never left their sights all night, must have used to make it happen.

Later, as he lay awake still wrestling with his thoughts, he heard the wizard downstairs talking to himself and rummaging around, and considered going down to see if anything was wrong. Then he thought more on this and decided not to, as he feared that his concern might not be appreciated by Garret or may even be misconstrued by him as interference. Once, when the night was at its most gloomy and hushed depths, he heard the squeaking sound of the cottage's front door opening and closing as if someone had gone out. It was sometime after that sleep finally swept over him and carried him to a twilight place where shallow images came and went and small figures danced to a haunting melody. Only when the light of dawn spread across the room from a dinky skylight window and he again heard the front door of the cottage opening and closing, did he jump from his sleep as if expecting to see someone standing over him, but found no one there. He thought then that it must have been the wizard going and coming and couldn't help questioning why many times before sleep enwrapped him again.

"Breakfast is ready!" called Garret heartily to stir all of them from their sleep that next morning. "Time to wake up and wash and fill our stomachs . . .and then we'll take to the road!"

"I'm so tired," complained Louise.

"Me too," yawned Maeve grumpily.

Padraig and Sammy were yawning also but said nothing as they rose up. Biddy, too, was yawning and went sleepily to the door to let out Penny and Pinch. They were bounding down the stairs when Garret called again from the hallway. "Come on now everyone! No time to lose! The food's going cold!"

A race began then that even left the wizard confused. He had just turned from calling them when a sudden burst of activity came from the upper room as Biddy and the children broke from it and took the stairs down past him. In a virtual whirlwind of arms and legs that left him flabbergasted, they scampered down to the breakfast table in the front room and began ravenously eating and drinking all that had been prepared for them. Smiling, but a little concerned that the biggest eggs and the largest pieces of bacon and the thickest slices of bread might all be eaten before he got any, Garret rushed to join them and began to eat and drink with as much enthusiasm as all of the others had put together.

An hour later when they had finished eating breakfast, Garret called them all around again to tell them about the journey that lay ahead and the possible dangers that they would be faced with before its completion. It wasn't that he wanted to unduly frighten them but more to ensure that they would be on their guard against the countless things that could go wrong on such a journey into the unknown. "If we stick together and watch out for one another, all will be okay," he said finishing, knowing that this would ease the concerns that all of them had as they prepared themselves to go.

There followed then what could only be described as a tremendous convergence of unusual and fantastic occurrences, whereby some unknown magic contrived to have all the cutlery and dishes washed, the chairs and tables straightened, the floors and windows cleaned, the household brass and silver and gold polished, every corner dusted and every surface shined, and all sorts of things put away in their proper places so that the cottage was at once spotless and as neat as a new pin. That all this was done in the blinking of an eye and the turning of a head was itself most improbable, but the fact was that neither Biddy nor the children saw any of it happening when they sat in its midst was even more incredible.

Once outside, the warmness of the old cottage seemed a memory as they trailed northwards away into a cold sunlit morning that held a low waltzing mist down on the fields. As they reached the beginnings of the further regions of the Great Northern Forest and saw for the last time the grey peaks of the Winterlan Mountains as they entered its woods, a silence descended on them that made them more aware of all the sounds of the deepening forest. Padraig and Sammy both had the same thoughts and it was with regard to food. Had the wizard remembered to bring any, and if he had (and there was no evidence to support this) was it enough to feed all of them for the rest of the journey? Yet neither of them said a word. They were getting used to things never being as they seemed when it involved Garret Dimple. Sammy though, had one question that he did want an answer to and feeling bolder than ever before, now that he felt he was getting to know the wizard better, he quickened his pace to join him.

"I was just wondering," he said politely.

Garret never broke his stride, but smiled wryly. "Wondering's a great thing."

"You haven't told us where we're going...not exactly anyway, and well, I'd like to know," persisted Sammy, suddenly not feeling so bold.

"We're going north," replied Garret, cautiously. "There's a wonderful place there called Sidhe Pool. It's a sort of fairy lake in the upper reaches of the Great Northern Forest. I'm hoping that we can find some help and some answers from a certain lady who resides there."

"Is it the Salmon Girl?"

"Yes. But there are no guarantees that she'll talk to us or even help us. She's been in hiding there for a long time now and is sure to be suspicious of all intruders."

"She sounds sad."

"Not so much sad, but perhaps broken by the things that have happened in the past and afraid of those waiting to happen in the future," said Garret profoundly. "As creatures, we recoil when we're threatened and seek out places of safety when we're afraid."

"But how do you know she's there?"

"I couldn't be sure that our friend Green, the leprechaun, was telling the truth when he told me where King Lugh was keeping your sister, and it was when I was playing with his mind a little and had him mesmerized so that he could only tell me the truth that I thought that he just might know where the Salmon Girl was hiding too, and he did. Even he doesn't know how helpful he's been."

"Is it dangerous at Sidhe Pool?"

"You've already experienced how dangerous all these northern parts can be when you entered the meadow of the giant flowers. See how our enemy can distort such beauty?"

A chilling shiver of dread ran through Sammy's body as he remembered. "But what if Largol is already there before us?"

"Sidhe Pool is an old place, governed by old laws that are beyond those of this world and any man or beast on it. Neither Largol nor I have any power over its sacred depths or the lady who dwells there. This far north, Largol will have his mark on everywhere else outside of the fairy lake though, and we can expect that he'll not give us easy passage to the places we need to go."

"Last night at your cottage...I heard you," recounted Sammy before a sudden severity in Garret's eyes made him hesitate.

"What about last night?" asked the wizard, calculating.

Sammy began to stutter. "I-I couldn't sleep and, and I, well, I thought I heard you talking to someone...and going out. And then later I heard you coming back. It was you, wasn't it?"

"You don't miss a trick, do you, little fella?" rasped the wizard, stopping completely in his tracks. "You should know better than to pay attention to the things that go on after dark, and that are of no concern to you!"

Sammy responded quickly. "I wasn't spying on you, honest. Sometimes when I think of all that's happened to my sister Dervla and the suffering it's caused our family, I find it hard to sleep. I didn't mean to listen to you last night, or to spy on you."

"We'll get Dervla back. Of that, I have no doubt," the wizard answered, turning to walk on again. "But there's a lot to do! A terrible lot to do!"

Consoled somewhat by the wizard's unflinching confidence that they would get his sister back, but still in need of an answer to a question that he was almost afraid to ask, Sammy went after him boldly. "What did the Mawlingfer do to you? Something's not right with you, something's missing. I'd like to know what it is."

"We all want to know," added Padraig, running to join them.

Then as the others moved nearer to see what was going on, Garret finally stopped. "I haven't been myself lately," he said, turning towards them and sidestepping onto a small mound. With the sunlight coming from behind where he stood, something which made his face seem sinister and gave his entire body an ominous silhouette, he threw open his cape and stretched out his arms and legs in a gaping x-shape. None of the others spoke but all of them had bemused looks on their faces. A confused moment went by. It was as if they were all dumbstruck in waiting for what would come next. Finally, Garret asked, "What do you see?"

"Has he gone mad or something?" Louise asked Maeve quietly.

"I said, what do you see?" asked Garret again, a demand in his voice.

Sammy, Padraig, and Biddy looked at one another as if baffled. Suddenly fearful of the wizard's cryptic question, they would have preferred to go on trekking rather than anticipate what they feared would be its terrible answer. Then, just like that, Sammy, seeing at last what was before his eyes and in that same gob-stopping instant, realizing just what was missing, came up with the answer.

"Your shadow! You've got no shadow!" he exclaimed.

"No shadow?" came the voices of the others. "It's impossible!"

"Look, his shadow's...not there," said Sammy, incredulously looking around. "Ours are, but not Garret's."

"The result of my run in with our friend, the Mawlingfer," confirmed Garret.

"He took your shadow?"

"The Mawlingfer's a creature from a place called Monn in the uncharted lands. Before they were a peaceful race, but now something's askew with them it seems. I've heard stories of a place in the uncharted lands where the spawn of demons and soul destroyers give shelter to many strange and horrifying aberrations of nature. Shadowtakers are just one of these aberrations. Somehow the race of the Mawlingfer have mutated, become the takers of shadows, a demon race that feed first on their victims' shadows and then on their very souls."

"But what does it mean...to lose your shadow? Do you feel sick, weak?"

Garret held his hand up into the sunlight to show that it cast no shadow. "Sometimes a wizard needs to send his shadow before him, and sometimes he needs to leave it behind. A wizard's shadow is his send-ahead scout and his leave-behind watcher, his companion and his fearsome defender in battle. A wizard's shadow can be a terrifying thing to those over ground and even worse for those under it. But without his shadow, a wizard's days are numbered. Slowly, its loss draws him out of his mind and his wits, until he becomes a dribbling wreck of a creature that finally loses not only his wizardry but even his very will to live. A ghost of his former self, he searches high and low, but finds no respite as even the memory of what he was searching for falls foul to his weakened condition. The light of day brings nothing but pain, and his only comfort is the darkness of night. It's as if somehow his shadow, for a brief interlude, comes back then. Many nightwalkers are those searching for their lost shadows, but few ever find them. Their searching goes on though, like an endless nightmare, until they finally lose their fight for life and surrender up their very souls."

Silence fell around the others then as they began to comprehend the trauma that Garret was going through.

Finally, Sammy asked. "Is that what you were doing last night then, searching?"

"Yes Sammy, that's all I was doing. It brings me a little peace and some much needed comfort."

Briefly, after they took off again, Garret could hear the others whispering amongst themselves about how sorry they were for him and how dismal his future looked, and he took exception to this, saying, "Hey, all of you! I don't need your pity! Save it for those who dare to cross swords with me and for those that have taken what's mine! I'll bring the heavens down on every last one of them!"

A long time went by then that saw them climbing high and low and trekking up and down and crossing and crisscrossing on lost forest paths that were wild and long and far. No one spoke again during that time. It was as though a single determination had taken hold of all of them, and it was to see the journey's end no matter what the consequences. Yet, at intervals, following strange creature-calls that echoed out from some uncultivated and astray depths of the forest's green darkness, they all began to experience fear.

When finally there came an opening through the trees, it was along the banks of the Silver River, a named given to it because its waters were the purest in all those parts. The river was shallow there, with calm pools circling in on themselves at a lazy bend where a fallen tree provided a natural bridge across to the other side. Garret was already resting there when the others, who had all fallen some way behind, arrived.

"Thought you had all gotten lost," he quipped cheerily, puffing on his pipe.

"I'm too old for all this trekking," complained Biddy as she shuffled into the opening followed by her cats.

"Stop complaining," said Garret. "We haven't got far to go."

Padraig, Louise, Maeve, and Sammy flopped down onto the river's grassy bank and stretched out as if to sleep. Indeed, they had just begun to enjoy the rest when Garret rose again and moved towards the fallen tree.

"It's time to cross," he said, looking up at the position of the sun.

"But we've only just got here," protested Louise.

"Follow on, quickly," ordered Garret, nimbly stepping up onto the trunk of the fallen tree to cross the river.

Louise was just about to argue again for staying there longer but stopped herself when all the others started to move. Standing there alone after they had gone, she felt an isolation that made her experienced just how slowly moments could pass when there is nobody there to share them with. This alone was enough to convince her to go after them.

CHAPTER 11

Once they had crossed to the other side, they left the Silver River behind and climbed out of its tree-lined valley to a winding pass that looked down onto another stretch of the Great Northern Forest where no roads or paths were visible and where whole tracks of the land were cloaked in a grey motionless mist. Moving stealthily, for there was an undeniable air of foreboding about the place that caused them to be extra careful and overly apprehensive, they clambered down a craggy scarp to a headland where the mist presented, what seemed to be, an impenetrable curtain before them. Yet not one of them shirked going forward. Even when Garret broke the mist's curtain when he entered it, causing it to open with a gnashing gape and swirl around and close behind as if to swallow him, they all still followed on without hesitation.

Further into its folds, the mist became thicker and darker under the shadows of the forest's trees. It was as though they were descending into an all-consuming black pit where the light of day had never reached. The only sounds were those of their own thrashing footfalls on the wet forest floor and some broken noises from deeper parts of the forest that could have been caused by the wind, had there been wind. Biddy, her cats, and the children walked on and on without really knowing what was before them or where they were going, yet they knew that Garret (who seemed as composed and as sure-footed as ever) would know for sure, and this kept them going. Before long, too, their faith in him was rewarded as the mist was given a golden glow when a sudden shaft of sunlight filtered through the trees and they caught their first sight of the deep blue waters of Sidhe Pool.

Louise and Maeve ran forward, shouting gaily. "It's beautiful! Just Beautiful!"

"Stay back!" warned Garret, halting them with an outstretched hand. "You're too full of noise! Too much noise is not the way of this place, understand?"

"Sorry, sorry," apologized the two girls sheepishly.

"It's a tender spirit we come to visit, and she doesn't appreciate loudness of any kind," whispered the wizard, as he pulled an enormous leaf from a tree and rolled it into a funnel.

"He's talking about the Salmon girl," realized Sammy with delight.

"Shush!" demanded Garret as the others began to stir. "Let's try something to make her come out into the open."

Watching Garret turning and shaping the leaf, Padraig was baffled. "What's he at?"

"He's making a horn, I think," guessed Sammy with a degree of uncertainty that vanished when Garret began to blow into the huge funnelled leaf.

The sound that went up was deep and hollow and one that sent a thousand ripples rushing out across the lake to a shore on the other side that was just visible beneath another bank of mist. The wizard blew the makeshift horn again and again, sending ripple after ripple across the watery divide until the ripples began to return, as if in reply.

"There," he said suddenly, putting the horn down as if something had been accomplished. Minutes later there was a rolling in the lake's waters. Suddenly, the surface was oozing with a bubbling concoction of movement, with silver crests going over and under and travelling out far and wide. In another moment, all went calm and a gentle wave broke on the shore near to where the children were. Just then, a girl's voice (with a higher pitch and a sweeter tone) repeated the sound that Garret had made with the horn.

"Is it you, Aoife?" asked Garret, and when no answer came he repeated softly. "Is it you, Aoife?"

Once more there was no answer, but almost instantly, the water began to churn again. Biddy and the children were fascinated, if a little frightened, for all they could see was a white shape rolling and turning deep within the lake's blackness. It looked like a gleaming seal or a brightly coloured otter but was unlike any that they had seen before. There seemed to be something almost human about its face and movements and, while they had had only fleeting glimpses of the creature beneath the veil of Sidhe Pool, they were all sure that what they were seeing was real and not some trick of the light's reflections on the lake's surface. They were still looking too, when the water went still again and calm circles broke outwards from where all the activity had been. They hadn't seen Garret stepping back and going to sit on a tree stump, or minutes later the exquisite, lithe creature that emerged from the other end of lake and went to sit with him. Sammy was first to spot them but was still half consumed by his hunger for another glimpse of the spectacle in the lake until he realized that it was now gone and that the lady sitting with Garret had that creature's face. Beckoning carefully to the others without making a sound, he directed their attentions towards the wizard and the exquisite creature who were both already engaged in deep conversation.

Louise's eyes were wide with questions. "It's the Salmon Girl, isn't it? It is, isn't it?"

"She's beautiful. Whoever she is," answered Biddy.

At once Maeve's face lit up. "Do you think she'll sing her song?"

Padraig was uncompromising. "We'll make her sing it! We haven't come all this distance for nothing!"

"The fairies won't need Dervla any more then," said Sammy hopefully.

As they moved closer, Biddy and the children heard Garret explaining to Aoife the whole escapade of the fairies taking Sammy's sister Dervla and replacing her with a changeling and the reason why and then of their ensuing efforts to get her back and of the various dangers they had encountered along the way. When he became aware that the others were nearby, he turned to them. "This is Aoife," he said, and then smiling jokingly, added to Aoife's embarrassment, "She's an angel, a spirit of the rivers and lakes and a guardian of the seas."

"Oh, would you stop it, Garret Dimple, please," moaned Aoife, holding back an embarrassed smile. "I'm no angel, far from it."

"And I suppose you're not the Salmon Girl of legend either?"

"I'm just plain Aoife now, that's all. I'm nothing special."

"But," protested Garret about to challenge her about why she was being so self-effacing when, to his surprise, she interrupted him abruptly.

"-Tell me their names."

"This is Sammy, the brother of Dervla, the girl who was taken," he continued, stuttering absentmindedly as a deathly whisper came across the afternoon forest. Of all of them there only Aoife and he had heard its threatening cry, for it was the calling out of his name by a cold distressed voice. "This is, eh, Biddy," he continued, "who some say is a witch. And these little ones are Louise, Maeve, and Padraig, friends of Sammy and his sister."

Aware, because of the desperate cry that something else was on Garret's mind and that it was probably for the best that Biddy and the children hadn't heard it, Aoife smiled graciously as they offered her their awkward hellos, saying, "You're all so brave to have come here."

"She doesn't look like a singer," said Maeve to Louise, a little too loudly.

"No, she doesn't, does she," agreed Louise.

"Will you two keep quiet?" rasped Sammy before saying to Aoife. "They didn't mean anything bad. You see we're just not used to seeing a...someone like you, I mean."

"It's okay, Sammy," laughed Aoife. "Really it is. You must all be tired trying to keep up with Garret. I'm sure he's had you marching at a terrible pace to get here."

"Running, more like!" wailed Biddy, kicking off her shoes and massaging the soles of her feet. "We've been travelling forever, and we've really only had just one night's proper rest. We've been up and down and over and under and on and on through every imaginable nook and cranny of the forest. It's a wonder we got here in one piece at all."

"It wasn't that bad, was it?" asked Garret.

"Yes, it was!" came a chorus of support for Biddy from the children.

"You're a hard task-master, Garret Dimple," smiled Aoife.

"Well now," responded Garret shrewdly, "hopefully it wasn't a wasted journey."

As if she already knew what he was going to ask Aoife pushed her silvery hair off her shoulders and back from her face with a graceful nonchalance that dispelled all the worries and troubles that Garret had brought with him. To her eyes there came an exquisite blue light that shimmered with a vision or some thought that he knew was beyond his comprehension, until he felt a delving into his mind, and it became clear that she was reading his thoughts. "Why do I hear your questions before you even ask them?" she asked then.

"But I've just one question."

"As you know, Garret, this place has its whisperers...and lately all the tales have been about you."

This caused a suspicious blaming glance from Garret towards Sammy, who shrugged his shoulders and recoiled acceptingly.

"You know my troubles then?" asked Garret.

"So many waiting on a song, depending on it," said Aoife, "and you know the consequences of my singing it?"

"I know, but why does it have to be this way? What cruelness takes a life when a song, albeit a special song that enhances life itself, is sung?"

"These are things we know nothing of. Our eyes are blinkered and our minds devoid of the capability to acquire that greater knowledge that can tell us why. All I know is that when I sing the song it demands that a life is taken by way of sacrifice. It's an old way, an old thirst that needs to be quenched if the curse is to be lifted from Lissendel and the fruits of the song are to be enjoyed to their fullest. The last time I sang the song I was convinced that it would be me who was taken, but it was to be a crueller sacrifice than that. My heart was broken in pieces when Andale gave up his life. This time I pray that it's my life that's taken, but there's no guarantee that it will be mine." Aoife paused then before quietly adding, with a wistful glance at

Biddy and the children to make sure that they were out of ear-shot, "It could be your life that's taken or one of theirs."

Garret's frustration bubbled over. "Is there nothing we can do to stop it?"

"Nothing. And there are no other options but to sing the song."

"These are grave times for Lissendel, grave times indeed. What will you do?"

"The summer is pushing on. Fish are waiting to come home to their spawning pools. They do this knowing that they are going to die, but that because of their deaths new life will break forth to fill the seas and rivers again. I've thought about singing the song, and I've thought about not singing it, and the consequences of both. Like the fish, I really wouldn't mind if it's my life that's taken so that new life will be given."

"I should have put a stop to all this the last time it happened," bemoaned Garret, "but I was too wrapped up in my own world and nothing else mattered."

"A burden gets heavier the longer you carry it. I should know. So let it go now."

Garret shook his head despairingly. "I can't do that. This time it stops. This time I'll rid Lissendel of the curse of Largol Despalt and his dark ways! And if I can't, I'll die trying."

"I've heard whispers about him, too," recounted Aoife. "He's brought together a dreadful band of the most atrocious renegades from the uncharted regions. He's moulded them into his very own likeness and sent them out scouring the countryside night and day in search of me. They've brought fear and desolation all across the places north of here. Now they're coming south. Soon they'll be here."

Garret's voice rose with violence. "They better pray that they avoid me! I'll cut everyone of them down where they stand!"

"There are too many of them, Garret and many more than even you could stand against."

"But you'll be safe here? The old laws that protect this place cannot be breached. Is that not true?"

Aoife drew herself in, a sudden shiver coming over her. "I don't know anymore. I came here to hide away from Largol and his type, and so far it's kept me safe. But new ways, new thinking, new magic, and new laws all challenge those that are old. So that even here I don't feel safe anymore."

"I'll get to Largol somehow!" exclaimed Garret in a fit of temper. "And I'll stop him! Without his leadership, his miserable motley vagabonds will disband and go their separate ways, of that I'm sure."

"It's too late for that," sighed Aoife, looking over the rippling lake, as if there might come on the small shiny crests of its waters a solution to their dilemma. "It's time for me to go and do what I have to. I haven't left here in over ten years, you know. In a way it's become my prison."

A quiet empathy came to Garret's face for a moment, before his eyes lit up. "Leave with us now then…"

Biddy and the children waited with mouths agape for Aoife's answer, but when a certain look of anguish grew on her face, they knew before she said a word that they would be leaving that place without her.

"I can't be responsible for another life taken," Aoife sighed, "and the nearer you are to me the greater the chances are that that will happen. I need to be alone when I sing the song so that there will be only one life there as an option for the sacrifice, mine."

Her sad and fearful voice disturbed Garret, but he decided not to pursue the matter any further just then, while quietly resigning himself not to give up on trying to find a solution.

As Aoife looked down at her own reflection in the lake, she began to experience an immense sadness. Suddenly to that place where the afternoon light had been teasing a golden sparkle from the crested plane of the lake, there came another strange swirling upheaval and a rash mixing of colours. Now Aoife was frightened, for in the very place where her reflection had been, there came another dark, growing semblance. She would have run too, or ducked under the deep opaque water in another part of the lake where there was safety, had there not come in that same confused instant, a feeling of something that was peculiarly familiar and warm and that she had long forgotten.

Still frightened however, she turned to go but stopped when she heard the loud whispering of her name and the sudden silence that fell on everything around after it. There had been animals foraging and bees buzzing and birds singing, but suddenly it was as if the whole place had stopped to listen.

"Is this your doing?" rasped Aoife, turning angrily on the wizard, but when her eyes met his, they directed her to look again towards the lake. Even Biddy and the children were at a loss to know what was going on. When Aoife turned again, the lake was settled and calm. Then came the whispering voice again, "Aoife...Aoife, come nearer."

Now desperate to understand what was happening, for this was a voice she knew or thought she did, she gingerly stepped back towards the water's edge and looked down to where her reflection should have been. Almost instantly, a small tremor broke over the lake from its centre and went out to the sides with widening watery ribbons that lapped against its shores with a soft white wash that rose and then retreated. As the lake drew its waters back to a single point where it bubbled over and opened up, all of the others backed away, as if expecting a further disturbance, leaving both Aoife and Garret frozen on the shore. In the place where Aoife's reflection had been, there was another face, a broad shimmering visage that was looking back at them and making motions as if to speak. Breathlessly, she fell to her knees, and then trying to wipe the image from her eyes because she was beginning to allow herself to believe it was real, she cried out and wept. "What is this, Garret?" she said. "If you're doing this, it's...it's cruel!"

"It's I, Andale," came the voice again.

"How can it be?" she cried, before shouting at Garret again. "Stop it! Stop it now!"

"You must not be afraid, my love," said the voice of Andale. "Sing the song. Make the fish swim to our shores again."

Aoife wept and shook her head with disbelief. "Is it you, really you, Andale, my love?"

"It's no trick of mine, Aoife," assured Garret, "I promise."

"Be the Salmon Girl once more," came the voice of Andale again, before fading with the words. "Sing your song, my love. Fear not...Fear not...Fear not..."

With that Aoife scrambled out into the water and swam up and down gracelessly searching for the image of Andale, but she could find nothing. Moments after, she came back to the bank and got out of the water, holding her head down in tearful despair. "Do I dare to dream, or was it nothing but the play of light casting shadows on the water and cruel whisperers from the woods making a fool of me?"

"I didn't do this, Aoife. I wouldn't," said Garret pleadingly. "And remember, I saw and heard what you did, and it was very real to me, too. Very real."

Aoife said nothing but walked a short distance away. In that time, Biddy and the children were becoming anxious, doubts filling their minds that she would still sing the song.

"You will sing the song, won't you?" Sammy asked Aoife suddenly. "I'm sorry, Miss...for the way that you feel, but you are our only hope. I don't know what we'd do to get my sister back if you refused to sing the song."

"Of course I'll sing the song, and we'll get your sister back, so don't worry any more now," smiled Aoife, holding back tears caused by the memories that had been brought back to her mind when she saw Andale's face in the lake and heard his whispering voice.

Garret, knowing the weight of her sorrow and feeling somewhat responsible for it, sighed then. "We'll need to know when you're going to sing the song."

"There's a full moon tomorrow night," answered Aoife. "I'll be at Linahen Rock, and at midnight, I'll sing my song. The fish have a liking for the full moon; some use it for guidance."

"What should we do till then?" asked Sammy.

"We're going to see King Lugh," said Garret.

Pointing out over the tops of some low-lying trees and beyond a patch of grassland to the north, Aoife explained. "Yes, go to Bunkleen Mount, the fairy mountain. It's that high blue mountain on the horizon where, in the right light, you can see the head of a stag. I believe the early morning light is the best time to see it. The very place you see the stag's head is where you'll find the entrance to the fairy kingdom. King Lugh is holding your sister there. Go to him and demand her release. But be careful, the old king will put up a fight to keep her. He's crafty and conniving and will probably try every trick he can think of to try to fool you. But tell him what's been happening. Tell him that I've come back and that I'm going to sing the song, but that I won't do it until your sister is freed. Tell him to light a fire on top of Bunkleen Mount tomorrow before midnight so that I'll know she's free. A fire that will be seen the length and breadth of Lissendel."

"Save he doesn't believe us?" questioned Sammy.

"Garret will make him believe."

This began a frantic phase of whispers and mutters amongst Biddy and children. Garret stood alone watching Aoife, but she never looked back at him. In a moment, before he realized it, she had waded back into the water and had gone under. It was only then when Garret became aware of a disturbance off to his left, where a flock of birds scattered suddenly on the wing and some smaller animals broke from the undergrowth of that same place that he realized that there had been a fear on Aoife's face as if she had become aware of an unfamiliar presence nearby. His suspicions roused, he inched forward, hushing queries from the others as to *what it was* before sliding his staff upwards into a firing position. The place again was silent and so much so that he even became aware of his own heart beating, its rhythmic thumps loud in his ears, almost too loud. For a moment it confused him and caused him to deny the other sounds that he began to hear, the ones that sounded like the clip-clops of a well-shod steed on the leafy forest floor before realizing, when a darkly clad rider bounded out from the place of the disturbance to quickly disappear over a rise to the north, that that's just what it was. Instantly, in his anger at being too late to react, he blasted a bolt of lightning from his staff into the nearby trees while shouting something in a language (unknown to the others) at the heavens in frustration. Finally, he calmed down and began to reason out the situation and to way up the possibilities. After all, he thought, the rider may have been an innocent passerby of no consequence. Perhaps it was only some wayward traveller making his way home or a stranger to those parts who had gotten lost on the unfamiliar paths. Yet, however he tried, he could not dismiss the possibility that it could have been someone more sinister: a rider sent by Largol to spy on them. If it was, and he had heard and saw everything that went on at Sidhe Pool that afternoon, he feared that there would be serious repercussions, for Largol would soon know that Aoife was going to sing her song, and he would be sure to try and stop her. Garret was still ruminating on these possibilities when the others gathered round him, their faces full of questions.

"It's nothing," he told them abruptly, not wanting to worry them. In his mind, however, he feared the worst.

CHAPTER 12

As the afternoon shadows deepened across the forest and darkness drew in all around, the whistling of a chill breeze was the only sound to accompany that of the group's trudging footsteps on the leaf-strewn path that led away from Sidhe Pool. To the children, the whole lush basin at that end of the forest had suddenly become unfriendly as the day sank under a creeping veil of greyness that was quickly bringing down the night. Distant on the horizon too, a growling bank of thunderous cloud rolled over the last light of the sun to bring a swelling plane of twilight that came much earlier than was normal to the sloping hills of the west. There was still light to the north however, where the highland silver crests of the ridges of Bunkleen Mount radiated with the almost mystical glow of an orange dusk. This served to fascinate the children and was a beacon for them, a shining light through the dimness that lifted their spirits and gave them hope and direction.

Biddy and her cats were too preoccupied with trying to catch up with Garret (who was again quickly leading them from the front with purpose and determination) to even look up at the wonderful play of the light on the fairy mountain. Garret had other things on his mind. There was the darkly clad rider that he'd seen earlier for one, but more imminent were those lithe shapes, other than shadows, that were swiftly moving parallel to them amongst the trees not far off, and then there were those small sparks of light caught up between the tangled woods that lay ahead, sparks that came on and off and others, as piercing as demons' eyes, that stayed on as if to watch their every step. Still Garret strode on, his staff at the ready for action. He had expected a reception of sorts from the old fairy king, and he even hoped that it was his trooping fairies that were the lithe shapes moving amongst the trees parallel to them and that it was they who were the owners of the sparks of light that went on and off (that he presumed were their keen blades and spears flashing in readiness for use) and that it was their piercing eyes that were watching their every move. It could have been a band of brigands, of course, that were waiting for their chance to attack, or a pillaging horde of outsiders that had travelled by sea to those shores from an unmapped land and were now ready to plunder. It also could have been some of Largol's riders, but he doubted this, believing that the rider he had seen earlier at Sidhe Pool was a more likely candidate. Largol had many riders but liked them to be inconspicuous, just faces in the mix of those of a crowd, sent out separately on missions where they would wait and spy. Ordinary men with ordinary faces, whose duties were to worm away from the inside at the places where they were stationed, watchers and listeners and waiters, ready to rise up at Largol's call. Of all these dangers, and especially if there was going to be fighting, Garret singled out King Lugh's trooping fairies as his preferred opponents, for even shadow-less, he knew his magic was more than a match for theirs. The brigands and outsiders he knew nothing of, and that he felt would have been a huge disadvantage to him. There was always the chance that they were under the rule of some powerful black-hearted wizard, with magic infinitely more superior to his. For as long as he could remember, there had been stories about such grisly raiders from far-flung places and unmapped lands that served under the devious manipulations of a wizard-lord and for years wreaked havoc on every place they went to build up his kingdom. Perhaps they were the same ones that were responsible for the fall from peace into discord and cruelty of the Mawlingfer of Monn, but only time would tell.

"Walk, walk, walk, and walk," moaned Biddy, as she came alongside Garret. "Is it any wonder I'm getting old before my time?"

"You see the way the path opens for us, Biddy, and how the lights show us the way?" answered Garret. "Inviting isn't it?"

"What do you mean? I see no path opening or any lights showing us the way."

A flare of menace came to Garret's face. "Maybe I'm imagining it then. Maybe those movements out in the trees along our flanks are caused by the wind. But is the wind strong enough to do that just now, Biddy? Maybe those sparks of light up ahead are moths caught in the last light of the sun or the first light of the moon. But where is the sun or the moon now to give the light?"

"You're right," gulped Biddy, peering through the half-light. "I-I see-see them now. What will we do?"

To Biddy, Garret seemed unconcerned. "It's not far to the base of the fairy mountain," he assured her. "We can settle there for the night. The children will be tired, so it's best if they don't know that we have company. I'll keep watch through the night so that our friends in the woods keep their distance. Don't worry. All will be fine."

"Glad you think so," mumbled Biddy, unconvinced.

Later at the base of Bunkleen Mount when they had made camp for the night and all was silent, sleep came quickly upon them all. Even Garret, who had been determined to keep watch and not to sleep, gave in to the soothing ambience of that place and succumbed to the trappings of a deep restful slumber. Had it not been for Biddy's cats, Penny and Pinch, there would have been no one left to watch, and there would surely have been a rash of consequences to be faced because of this. For on many occasions throughout the night, when those lithe figures in the trees seemed just footsteps away and the sparks of light that were ahead had approached nearer than ever before, it was only the felines' vigilance — a disciplined schedule of circling about the camp with their backs arching and mouths snarling — that kept them at bay.

When morning came and the danger had dissipated, Garret awoke just moments after Penny and Pinch had finally settled down to sleep. He stirred at first, yawning and stretching and a little confused for some seconds before suddenly realizing where he was and why.

Quickly, he rose and grasped his staff to stand guard. "Where...? Why...?"

Biddy began to stir too, when she heard the commotion. "Is it morning already? You've been awake all night, Garret Dimple. Well done!"

"Eh, yes, well…indeed," spurted Garret, awkwardly accepting the undeserved praise.

Biddy went to where Penny and Pinch lay then. "Come on you two lazy fleabags. Time to get up!"

The cats were meowing lazily when the children woke too. A little way off, Garret was already searching the near horizon of Bunkleen Mount when sunlight began to creep over its slopes. The air was cold in the shade where the children had been sleeping, and when they began to complain about this, they looked to see where Garret and Biddy were. When they finally spotted the wizard and the witch, a hushed astonishment passed between them. Garret was standing outright on a rock, his hand raised to stop Biddy moving any further forward; silhouetted by early golden sunlight, both of them were looking upwards as if frozen in the presence of something unusual.

Sammy was first to break from the shade into the sunlight. "Look! Look up there!"

"It's the stag's head!" came a collective response from the others when they too, left the shade.

"And it's not that far up. We'll be there in no time."

As they moved forward, a new resplendence came over the sky, and all the darkness that had been there was overtaken by the new light of morning. Then suddenly, the sun rose fully with a magnificent blast that sent huge rays of light across Bunkleen Mount and blinding flashes out in every direction over the forest and the whole base of the valley. When the children, blinded momentarily by the brilliance of the sunlight flashes, looked again, the stag's head was gone.

Padraig's eyes were squinting to see. "Where's is it, the stag's head?"

"It's gone. We'll never find the entrance to the fairy mountain now," answered Louise.

"Wait!" cried Maeve, intensely listening. "Can you hear the singing? It's Dervla, I tell you! Dervla!"

Sammy smiled as he listened and moved to and fro with excitement, as if following the sound of the voice through the air. He would have danced with joy had the singing continued, but as quickly as it rose so, too, did it die. He was left deflated and somewhat confused but soon perked up again when Garret came back to where he was and shouted to them all. "Quick, gather round! They're coming to meet us!"

Sammy saw them then: a winding line of diminutive riders that were moving down and spreading out from an opening in Bunkleen Mount near to where they had seen the stag's head just minutes before.

"It's the trooping fairies," whispered Biddy. "Be on your guard, Garret Dimple..."

Garrett was looking off to the side at something that concerned him more than the sudden emergence of the trooping fairies. Over on the western side of Bunkleen Mount an ominous swirling form had begun to grow. It wasn't that it was of such enormous proportions that worried him so much because it was rather small, but that it was so dark and full of a potent energy that made it churn and jump and move at sudden terrifying speeds. Cautiously, he watched its progress as it moved to the left and to the right, rasping down on the gritty slopes and cutting every obstacle from its path regardless of whether it was a tree or a boulder, while all the time moving menacingly closer to where they were.

Garret was prepared for a fight, and it looked as though that that was just what he was going to get, for by the time the black whirlwind got to where he was, the trooping fairies had arrived on either side and had spread out in a semicircle with their arms at the ready. Still Garret stood tall, and when he held out his flashing staff, his whole body seemed to grow in bulk until it resembled what could only be described as a convergence of the most frightening beast of the forest and that of a vengeful angel. Even Biddy and the children moved away from him and huddled together when they saw the fierceness in his eyes.

"Stand where you are!" he ordered them, swinging his staff. "If the old king wants a fight I won't disappoint him!"

Suddenly the vicious swirling form was there before him, jumping and spinning portentously with all its black menace.

Garret arched himself and made ready to fight. "Are you first then to challenge me? Come on! Come and get it, dust-devil!"

"Not I," came the reply from a voice within the swirling form, followed by a long lazy whoosh that suggested it was slowing down.

Garret remained alert nevertheless. "Who speaks?"

Spinning slower and slower, the swirling form seemed smaller and less of a menace suddenly. At its centre, there was a core which, as it spun less and less, began to take on the appearance of a small brightly dressed man.

"Give me your name, or I'll cut you in two!" demanded Garret impatiently.

"It is I, Dartradisadene, at your service," answered the small man, while at the same time performing a cartwheel and a somersault that propelled him completely out of the swirling form, causing it to disappear and leaving him standing impertinently before Garret, offering him his hand in friendship.

Garret never moved to take his hand but only eyed him disdainfully. "You look like some clown to me, little fellow."

"I do?" sneered Dartradisadene, his eyes deliberately gloating with the awareness of how surrounded and outnumbered Garret and the others were by the trooping fairies. "And will you not you take my hand in friendship, Mister...Garret Dimple, isn't it?"

"I want to see the old king," demanded Garret.

Frustrated, Dartradisadene walked a small circle to make his point. "Ha! Just like that! I want to see the old king! Do you, really? King Lugh's...busy, busy, busy. Understand? That's why I've come to see you."

"And this rabble?" answered Garret, causing some of the trooping fairies' horses to rear up when he pointed his staff at them.

"They're the King's guards. He has a many enemies. You could be one."

"You should pray that I'm not..."

"My hand is still out to you," said Dartradisadene cunningly, before turning to Biddy and the children. "Maybe one of your friends will take my hand."

"Don't take his hand!" shouted Garret fiercely when Sammy moved to do so. "Don't take his hand...not unless you want to be a fool like him, an Amadawn!"

"What...but?" cried Dartradisadene, but his efforts to protest were quickly smothered when the sheep-hook end of Garret's staff fastened around his neck, and he was spun through the air like a shot in a sling.

Garret growled. "Friendship you want, is it?"

"Y-y-yes! Y-y-yes!" squealed Dartradisadene as Garret spun him round faster and faster.

"Knowing that if I took your hand I'd become an Amadawn too!"

"Yes. But I had no choice, you see. King Lugh sent me to stop you. He knows that you're here to take the girl, Dervla, back and he's not going to let you. I'm just a poor clown who was doing his duty."

Garret stopped spinning him when he heard this. "And the girl, is she in good stead?"

"Yes. She's singing better than ever, that is until she tries to sing the *Song of the Salmon Girl*. Something's not right or missing when she sings it. But the king says that her voice is getting better and better all the time."

"The old king should know that no mortal could ever sing that song!"

"Indeed. Don't say that I said it, but even an Amadawn like me knows that!"

Garret looped his staff off Dartradisadene's neck then, but was careful to keep him at a distance. "Take us to see the king. And let there be no tricks, or I'll make you pay!"

Glad to be released, the Amadawn gulped desperately for air. "Sure...of course, and I promise there'll be no tricks. You're a feared man in these parts, Garret Dimple, and I don't want any trouble with you."

"Lead on then," ordered Garret, waving to Biddy and the children to fall into line behind, as the trooping fairies broke from the circle that they had formed around them to flank out on either side. There was something about being hemmed in on both sides by the trooping fairies that made Biddy's cats,

Penny and Pinch, uncomfortable. They followed her for a short time only and, when they saw their chance, trailed off behind to eventually slip away into undergrowth where they followed and observed the others from a safe distance.

Chapter 13

They had only a short way to climb from the sparse forest at the base of Bunkleen Mount to the trimmed scarp and gritty slopes where a natural rock formation (that with the right combination of light and shadow had the silhouette of a stag's head) jutted out over a small grotto that was the entrance to the fairy kingdom of King Lugh. Garret had expected a grander entrance and was somewhat disappointed when he had to stoop through a low arch and push along a narrow tunnel before it opened up into a larger cavern. Even then, there was nothing special or spectacular about the entrance. It was just one vast hole that was dripping and damp and dark and that led to another that was almost identical, and had it not been for a small light at the far end of its blackness, there would have been no reason to suspect that it was the entrance to another world. Yet when they moved nearer to the far end of that same disturbing gloom and the small light began to grow, it became clear that there was an opening there that had been designed purposely so as to conceal it from the outside world.

Suddenly, the dark hill had opened up into a wide promenade with gilded paths and crystal walls and ornamented columns of gold and silver. Beyond this, there was an exit out again (as if to the other side of Bunkleen Mount, yet it was within the mountain) that led onto an undulating pasture that had such a rich and lush texture of green that it must have been a new and previously undiscovered shade of that colour. Above, from a cloudless blue sky, a warm but never burning sun shone over a gently rolling landscape that was dotted with uniform clutches of emerald forest through which a green and blue river meandered lazily. Further off, on a hump-backed hillside where the amazing colour of green that was all around became another deeper shade that somehow sparkled from within, there lay a fortified palace the grandeur of which was unsurpassed by any in the mortal world. So great was its splendour that it left Garret opened-mouthed with wonder, and for minutes almost overwhelmed Biddy's senses and those of the children.

Louise was truly impressed. "It's more beautiful than...than anything I've ever seen."

So too, was Maeve. "Are we inside Bunkleen Mount, or have we come out the other side?"

"It's another world," gaped Sammy.

"The fairy kingdom," added Padraig in awe.

Garret came to his senses when he saw the gates of the ramparts at the side of the palace opening and another troop of battle-clad (and, he thought, sterner) fairy riders emerging and coming to meet them. "Enough of this. Business waits to be done!"

In minutes, they were surrounded on all sides by the diminutive troops, the original ones on either side and the sterner ones filing in behind and out in front. Nothing was said as they went forward. Garret was still striding out as boldly as ever to let them all know that he was ready for any trouble that might happen and that he was undaunted by their numbers. Dartradisadene, on the other hand, was carefully picking his way forward, as if afraid to look back and always mindful that Garret was there behind him with his terrifying staff.

A greater troop still, awaited them when they reached the great gilded arches that rose over the palace's enormous courtyard and another as they proceeded on to enter it. There, the old king waited, sprawled on a solid gold, diamond encrusted throne like a fat doleful toad that would eat his own and show little remorse. His face was red, and his stomach wide, and he had an impish look about him and a distinct lack of royalty that made Garret quietly consider that he may have been just another Amadawn and to question (albeit to himself) whether he should be sitting on a throne at all.

Dartradisadene wheeled round when they went before the old king and then bowed before him, saying, "Garret Dimple, the wizard, and...and his companions, Your Majesty. They're here because...because —"

"I know why they're here, you idiot!" growled the king. "But why are they still here? Did I not tell you to...discourage them, to send them away, specially the wizard? Why, oh why, am I surrounded by such ineptitude?"

Garret pumped himself up defiantly and before Dartradisadene, who was cowering in the presence of the old king, could say anything, said boldly. "Your Majesty, King Lugh, did you really think this Amadawn and this sad rabble that you call troops could stop me coming here?"

"You'd be wise not to start trouble with me, Mister," warned the king, threateningly. "You haven't seen my troops fighting yet!"

"Largol Despalt started all this, remember that. It was him and his black conjuring that caused the fish to stop swimming before, and now he's done it again. Have you forgotten? Can you not see that he wants to rule all the known regions of Lissendel below and above ground, your world and mine? He's the one you should take arms against. But if you want to fight me, I'll gladly accommodate you!"

The king laughed and coughed and laughed and coughed again, finding this extremely preposterous, but amusing. "You're a character, Garret Dimple, a character indeed! You'll fight them all, will you?"

Instantly Garret threw open his cape and locked his eyes firmly on the old king, warning him, 'Yes – but you'll be the first to fall!'

Not wanting his troops to see him back down, the old king bent forward towards Garret and whispered, "I'm sure we can come to some arrangement, Mister. But what will we do about this Largol fellow who wants to rob me, us, of what's mine, ours, I mean?"

"Leave him to me."

"So it's fisticuffs between you and him then?"

"If you want to put it that way," smiled Garret.

"Hmmm," groaned the king, deep with thought. "Knew his father, Largol's. Old Han Despalt, the wizard supreme. Don't know what's become of him. He was a mysterious type, a nasty individual too, an avaricious taker who would cut you in pieces just to test his blade and who would take your last penny just to add one more to his own coffers." Then laughing, he added, "Apart from that, he wasn't a bad sort!"

Garret couldn't help himself laughing for a moment, but soon came to his senses. "You know the girl can never sing that song, don't you?"

"Here underground things are...different," whispered King Lugh, careful that his voice would not be heard by anyone other than Garret. "The natives are a demanding, restless bunch that always need to have something to look forward to. They really are no use when it comes to hardship of any sort, you know. All this talk of there being no fish in Lissendel's rivers and of none coming home to our shores this year and of the likelihood of the crops failing...well, it's enough for them to start questioning my, how-do-I-put-it, stewardship of this blessed realm. When Aoife, the Salmon thing-Girl, went missing, I didn't know what to do."

"So you took the first young girl with a voice that you came across to try to fool your own people into believing she was the Salmon Girl?" asked Garret.

"Not true. I've taken many a girl, but none of them had the voice that I sought, so I let them go. I've watched the girl, Dervla, for a long time. She has a...mystical voice, you'll agree, a great talent. Given time, her voice will only get better, you know."

Garret's face creased with frustration. "But it will never be good enough to master the *Song of the Salmon Girl*! Surely you knew that?"

The king shifted wearily, gesticulating with both hands to move back some of his soldiers and servants who had strayed too near to where they sat, while eyeing the others there to confirm that they were out of earshot. "Being a king is a huge responsibility," he continued. "It's all about image, how you look, not how you feel. It's not about what you do, really, but what you say you'll do. Many a king has been overthrown for doing nothing, and yet many others have become legends on the backs of promises that never came to fruition. It's lonely being the king."

"What do you think will happen to you when they find out that the girl can never sing the song?"

The king looked around then, fearfully. "I don't know, is the answer. Perhaps it's just bought an old king some time to think and to prepare for when he is no longer king. Look at them all feeding off me, watching my every move, every minute of the day. Whispers come to them too, you know. I can tell that some of them suspect that the girl's not the real Salmon Girl but maybe my trying to deceive them has accidentally brought good fare to my door."

"What do you mean?"

"Some say you're a great wizard whose abilities know no bounds," retorted the king, cunningly. "Of course, there are some who say that you're just a washed up magician who is in the twilight of his days and whose so-called abilities are just a pack of theatrical tricks!"

Garret's face was expressionless. He knew the king was fishing for some weakness in his reaction. "Really? And what do you say?"

The king paused a minute. "I say that you go and find Largol and put an end to him and what he's doing. Sure wouldn't that prove to all your doubters that you are as great as some say you are. We don't really need a sad old song to be sung to stop what's happening, do we?"

"Only the song sung by the real Salmon Girl will stop what's happening!"

The king yawned dismissively. "Enough! The deal is, you rid us of Largol and the girl goes free! If you don't, she doesn't... Got that, magician?"

Biddy and the children were frozen with fear and looked to Garret warily. Garret, though, remained staunch as he readied his staff, his eyes fixed with contempt on the old king. "How long do you think it would take your troops to take me down? Five-minutes? Ten minutes? An hour? It will only take me one brief instant to blast you to a new kingdom all of your own!"

"You're certainly a big talker, Mister," laughed the king with a huge gulp of nervous laughter, before adding, "But are you and your little bunch not my prisoners at this very moment?"

Garret beckoned to Sammy to come forward. "You've taken this lad's sister from her family. I've come to take her home."

Again, the king laughed, and this prompted the trooping fairies to join him. "I suppose you want all my treasure too and my throne?"

"Give me the girl, and you'll have no trouble," answered Garret, a distinct threat in his voice.

The king was equally threatening. "Look around at how out-numbered you are! Now can four children, a scrawny old witch and you, a washed-up, shadow-less wizard match up to my army? I don't think so."

Garret was stumped for a moment but kept his composure and said nothing, aware somehow just then that his silence presented a far greater threat than would any words.

"Yes," confirmed the king, "I've heard about your trouble with the Mawlingfer of Monn. All of Lissendel knows by now, and Largol too, I should think."

"We've seen Aoife, the Salmon Girl," said Garret finally. "I've talked to her. She'll sing the song for us, but only if you let the young girl go."

"Don't try to trick me, wizard," rasped the king, angrily. "The Salmon Girl's gone missing. She may even be dead. Nobody's seen her in years. You're lying!"

Suddenly Garret raised his voice so that everyone there could hear him. "You're the only liar here! You even lied to your own people! You're not a king. You're an Amadawn!"

The king reacted furiously, roaring loudly before any of his men could question what it was that Garret was talking about. "Put them in chains! Throw them in the dungeons!"

Sammy broke loose then. "You've taken my sister! Let her go now!"

"No chance!"

As the trooping fairies drew their weapons and began to advance, Garret threw off his cape and flung it into the air.

Everyone stopped as it began to fall and spread out, for there was a sinister glowing form materializing in its centre and growing outwards, a dark-eyed crimson creature that snapped and snarled and threatened. Within seconds, it had begun circling protectively around Biddy and the children, spitting and swiping in such a ferocious and terrifying way that it formed an impassable barrier that the fairies were unable to penetrate. Before the king had time to react, Garret swung round and aimed his staff at him. The king ducked sideways and went to move away but was stopped going forward by a vicious dagger of lightning that shot from Garret's staff and landed at his feet. Garret watched for a moment then, saying nothing. All around him there was panic, and now the trooping fairies were advancing on him. In the king's eyes, there was only menace. Garret knew that if he showed any weakness just then they would all be done for, so he shot another lightning bolt above the heads of the trooping fairies and then turned again on the old king.

"Call them off!" he shouted, aiming his staff directly at him. "Call them off or the next shot goes between your eyes!"

The king shivered with the thought and then grimaced nervously before smiling as if he was greeting a friend. "We've got off to a bad start, got our lines crossed. I mean, you and I both want the same thing—to see the fish swimming again, do we not?"

Garret knew the king was playing for time. "Listen, you old buzzard. I'll blast you where you stand if you don't call them off now!"

"Okay! Okay! Relax! Relax! I'll call them off," answered the king uneasily, but before he could issue the order for the trooping fairies to pull back he heard Dartradisadene shouting, "Fire!" and moments later saw a hail of arrows descending on Garret. Then, as he watched Garret somersaulting across the courtyard to avoid being hit by the arrows and saw him losing his grip on his staff and dropping it, he laughed slyly and said with some degree of satisfaction, "They are an impetuous bunch..."

Surrounded by the advancing troops, Garret rose bravely and prepared to fight, his shape changing to that of a terrifying forest beast. Biddy and the children were still being protected from attack by the creature that came from Garret's cape, but the fairies were advancing on them too, and they were beginning to fear the worst. It was when all seemed lost and just as Garret and the others were about to be overrun by the hordes of trooping fairies that the two bounding figures of Biddy's cats, Penny and Pinch, broke through the ranks of the surprised and suddenly frightened fairies to pounce on the king and pin him down. Garret had already waded through fifty of trooping fairies, casting them aside like broken toys and throwing them back on themselves in bloody heaps. He was conjuring up all sorts of unsightly spectres too, to frighten them, and packs of roaring beasts that caused them to break their lines. It was most likely that he would have single-handedly (with the aid of his terrifying illusions) defeated the whole army of trooping fairies, had not the king, a writhing ball of confusion under the threat of Biddy's snarling cats, called, "Stop! I give up! We give up!"

"But I'm only starting to enjoy myself," quipped Garret.

The king didn't find this funny though. "You can have the girl. Just get these...these beasts off me!"

Garret stroked his chin ponderously and then shook his head. "And I'm to trust you?"

"I'll give you my treasure, too," bawled the king.

"Keep your treasure. Just release the girl."

"Okay, okay! Now get these infernal felines off me! How I detest the smelly creatures!"

Garret picked up his staff and readied it to fire and then nodded to Penny and Pinch to let the old king up, warning him, "Any tricks and you'll get it between the eyes. Understand?"

"There'll be no-no t-tricks," stuttered the king, before shakily summoning two guards and telling them to release Sammy's sister, Dervla.

"And for what it's worth, what I said about the Salmon Girl is true," explained Garret, "whether you believe me or not. I've talked to her, and she will sing her song. All the time that she's been missing she's been staying not far from here. In fact, she's been right under your nose, in Sidhe Pool."

"Sidhe Pool? Our sacred lake? Never!"

"And she'll sing her song this very night once you release the girl."

Still the king was not convinced. "I'm not arguing with you any more, wizard. You're deluded. You'd say anything to get the girl back. Well, you can have her. I'll find another singer, another Salmon Girl."

"He's telling the truth," Sammy said, a plea in his voice.

"Light a fire up on top of Bunkleen Mount tonight before midnight," Garret added, his eyes firmly engaging those of the old king. "One that will be seen across the whole valley. Aoife, the real Salmon Girl, will sing her song when she sees it. It's the sign she's asked for to let her know that the girl has been released. She'll only sing the song if she sees the fire. Take my word on it."

When the two guards brought Sammy's sister Dervla forward, it was as though she had been released from a dream. "Is that you, Sammy? Where am I?"

"We've come to take you home," cried Sammy, hugging Dervla affectionately and almost tearful with disbelief that they had finally got her back.

Biddy and the other children gathered round Dervla and Sammy then, shouting jubilantly and joyously hugging them.

Slowly Dervla's eyes began to focus on where she was. "The last thing I remember I was playing with you, Maeve. I could hear...music, the strangest and most beautiful music ever. Then everything went blank."

Maeve was trying to hold back tears of joy. "It doesn't matter. You're safe now, and we going to take you home. That's all that matters."

"I keep trying to sing this song too," continued Dervla, her voice agitated and hoarse. "It's such a strange song that it makes my voice hurt. But I can't seem to stop trying to sing it. What does it mean?"

"Forget about it, Dervla. We're taking you home!" said Louise.

"You wouldn't believe the trouble you've caused us!" complained Padraig, before then realizing what he had said and adding, "But it wasn't your fault. Really, it wasn't."

Dervla was still confused. "What trouble? What wasn't my fault?"

Biddy placed an arm around Dervla's shoulders then and took her to one side. "I'll explain all that's happened to you." Then, as she began to detail how Dervla, some weeks before, had been abducted by the king's fairies while playing near the fairy rath at Lushly Fields, Maeve, Louise, and Padraig came round where they were and listened intently as if the story was new to them too.

Garret was still keeping his eyes fixed doggedly on every movement of everyone around them when Sammy approached the old king. "King Lugh. Your Majesty," he said, "Garret's telling you the truth. It's true that we wanted my sister Dervla back and that we would have done almost anything to make that happen, but we also want the fish to come back to our rivers again, and we don't want the crops to fail. In Creel, where we live, almost every man is either a fisherman or a farmer. Garret's right, only Aoife, the real Salmon Girl, can sing the song. And she'll sing the song tonight at midnight, once she sees the light of the fire from Bunkleen Mount. Please believe us."

"Because I'm a fair and honest man," said the king loudly in an effort to save face in front of his trooping fairies, "I'll give you the benefit of the doubt. Not because I'm an old fool who likes to believe in the fantastic, or because I'm afraid of your friend, Garret Dimple, remember that. Tonight I'll light the biggest fire that's ever been seen on Bunkleen Mount! Take it as an apology from me to you and your family for taking your sister away."

"Thank you, Your Majesty! You won't be sorry. I promise you won't."

Then the king turned to Garret. "Are you sure this is Aoife, the real Salmon girl, the one that's been missing, and that she'll sing the song?"

"As sure as can be."

"I wouldn't be so certain that she'll get to sing her song, if I were you," said a voice from the ranks of the trooping fairies that parted almost instantaneously to reveal the speaker's identity. It was the leprechaun, Green.

"Who speaks?" asked the king, peering through the crowd, before finally seeing Green. "Is that you, Green, the keeper - leprechaun - thing of Linahen Rock? How's my gold?"

Green came forward into the light then. "Yes it's me, Green, Your Majesty, and your gold's fine."

"So what do you mean with the *'I wouldn't be so certain that she'll get to sing her song if I were you'* business? Come on," sighed the king, impatiently. "Come on! Speak!"

"I know these children and their plight," continued Green. "As for the old witch and her cats, I've made it my business to avoid them. Garret Dimple, too, the great wizard; I've always thought it wise to give him a wide berth. But now I find myself embroiled in all this trouble with them, and there's little I can do about it."

"What do mean, you're embroiled in all this trouble with them? You seem to know something that I should. You don't believe that the Salmon Girl, Aoife, will sing her song, do you? Why?"

"Forgive me, Your Majesty," croaked Green, his eyes lost on the things he was remembering.

The king exhaled impatiently. "Oh, for what?"

"I should have come to you earlier, but something came over me, a fear that I never had before. You see I've known all along where the Salmon Girl was."

"You, you knew and never told me!" rasped the king. "You knew where she was all along while I was sending out riders up and down the countryside night and day trying to find her! You knew while I was grasping at nettles trying to find answers! I could have your head for this! Why didn't you tell me?"

"For years now, Your Majesty, a great miserable greed has slowly been taking hold of me, coursing through my veins like an all-devouring snake."

"What have you done?"

"So much so," continued Green, "that I was unable to eat or sleep. A day would disappear into another and another into another and all I could think of and dream of and see was the glow of my gold, my dear gold—"

"Your gold?" laughed the king. "You don't have any gold!"

"I mean, your gold! You understand, you do understand?" Green paused then as if waiting for a look of understanding from the old king, but when none came he again continued. "Before I knew it, I was full of dark deeds, unwholesome thoughts and black, black machinations. I wanted the gold, your gold to be mine! The years I spent looking after it have taken their toll. The endless days and nights of minding it and protecting it haunted me so relentlessly that my every waking thought was filled with its golden beauty and its yellow peril, until finally it took possession of my mind and my body. It will do that to you after a time. You see all I had of a dark night was the glow of your gold, my gold, and on a cold one the feel of it. Just to look at it kept me going in the darkness and warmed me when it was icy."

"So tell me what have you done?" repeated the king, a noticeable tone of indifference in his voice that Garret found strange for someone who was hearing an unfolding story with a certain inevitability about it that made it seem that his gold had gone missing or had been, at the very least, at risk of having been taken.

"I wish I could change everything that's happened..."

"Oh, stop moaning and tell us what's happened!"

Green went on despondently. "One day in the great forest I came across a man, a gentle old man it seemed, who had a fondness for the game of casting coins. Like a fool, I was drawn into a game that only a magician or a wizard can win. We played for small change at first, and I found it unusually pleasant and enjoyable even. You see he let me win the first round of games and this, feeding a greed that I never knew I was capable of until I played the game, made me bolder with the stakes. In an hour, I went from wagering small money to risking all that I owned... and then, yes, even your gold! I was sure the old man would tire before long, but he never did. Maybe I was a little drunk at the time. No, I was just greedy. When I began to lose, I kept thinking that I'd beat him the next time and the next time... but it never happened. Finally, I was clean broke. I'd lost all my money and all of yours, Your Majesty, every gorgeous yellow coin of your treasure!"

"My treasure? My treasure? Ha! You think that I'd let some stinking leprechaun like you watch over my treasure, my gold?" chuckled the king, avariciously. "My gold is my own, my very own! It's guarded by an unconquerable legion and locked away in an impregnable chamber in a bottomless pit beneath an un-scalable mountain on an unmapped island where it basks in its own warm glow. My gold is for nobody's eyes but mine, only mine! You hear? I used you as the keeper of my false treasure to avert the eyes of greedy fortune seekers from the real treasure. You were nothing but a foil guarding a pile of worthless yellow coins. You served your purpose, but that you even thought to gamble with my false treasure is a worry for me that makes me demand retribution!"

"It wasn't real?" came Green's incredulous response.

"Not a coin of it!"

"Who was this old man that you met in the forest?" inter-jected Garret.

"He must have known that the gold wasn't real too," pon-dered Green, "while I like a fool never suspected it. That's why he made me an offer that I couldn't resist. Only now can I see how it's made things worse for everyone."

The king's patience began to wear down. "Tell us what you've done, Amadawn!"

"He promised to give back all that I'd lost – my gold," Green continued sheepishly, correcting himself with a shake of his head as his mind still wrestled for the ownership of the gold. "I mean your gold, when I'd completed a series of errands for him. But the errands he had in mind were of a devious nature the likes of which required that I walk in the shadows to spy on those who were trying to do good. I had to listen to things that were not for my ears and whisper stories that were laced with lies, all as a ransom for those yellow shiny coins of gold. Even now I run for him in the hope that he'll finally give me back what's mine, yours, I mean. I know now that I've been a fool."

It all sounded too familiar to Garret. "The old man was Largol in disguise, wasn't it?"

"Only when I agreed to his terms did he reveal himself to me in all his gluttonous revelry. His ambition is boundless and his ruthlessness a thing to be truly feared. The true weight of my burden and the malicious nature of the acts that I would be required to carry out were lost to me then, but now I see my errors clearly, and I'm willing to pay for my mistakes. Stop him before he rules all! Stop him before he ends our days with his dark plans! But be careful. His agents are everywhere. There are many out above ground and even more here in our midst below it. Largol—ahhh!'

Without warning a furore went up from within the ranks of the trooping fairies as several fiery arrows were shot from hidden bows to cut through the air and fall on Green. There and then, clutching the one arrow that found and pierced his chest, Green stumbled forward with an agonizing sigh and fell. Garret rushed to his aid for a minute but then got up and pushed his way into the middle of the trooping fairies, causing them to spread outwards.

"You want trouble?" he said, swinging his staff (that had become a shining sword), around in a great cutting arc. "Come on, you cowards. I'll give you trouble! Fight me! Show yourselves! Show me your fiery arrows!"

This caused the trooping fairies to push back and spread out even further, as if most of them had expected the culprits to come forward, but nobody did. Garret waited a short time too for someone to show, then somewhat frustrated, returned to Green, who was now beginning to lose consciousness. The children and Biddy had gathered there too.

"He's starting to fade," whispered the king, before moving closer to Green to ask, "Are you still with us, Green?"

"Largol is onto what you are trying to do," croaked Green, pulling the old king into him as he continued the sentence that he had begun before the arrows were fired. "By now, he'll be racing to Linahen Rock to stop the Salmon Girl singing her song. Your Majesty, she is the real one, and it's true that she's coming out of hiding. When she sings her song, everything will be reversed, normal again. The fish will swim, and the crops will grow! Tonight before midnight, she'll come ashore near Linahen Rock. Light the fire! She must sing her song! But Largol knows this, and he's sworn to stop her. You mustn't let him!" Green coughed then and tried to push himself upwards but was unable to.

"Rest now," whispered the king, Green's dying words finally making him believe that the real Salmon Girl had returned.

"His plan is to lord it over all of Lissendel, both above ground and here below it, and he'll succeed if he's not stopped," coughed Green before turning to Garret to confess. "The rider at Sidhe Pool this afternoon...it was me. I've always been clumsy when it comes to horses. I've been following you, spying on you for Largol ever since you came to see me at Linahen Rock. He knows your plans and will try with all his might to upset them. I'm so sorry...I only wanted my gold back...but now even that doesn't matter. Forgive me..." Then beckoning weakly to Garret to come nearer still, he said softly, "*Phoularnacrushnaparteenthomond!* Use it when it seems all is lost. Use it, too, wisely."

Garret went to ask for more information from Green as to when and where to use the word, but before he could, the leprechaun's eyes closed for the last time.

"There's still time," said Garret to the others urgently. "If we move quickly, we can make Linahen Rock before Largol." Then he shouted to Biddy and the children. "Come on. Let's get going!"

The king stood boldly then, finally a believer. "I'll send my troops to help you."

"No!" responded Garret. "I wouldn't know who to trust amongst your troops. Look what they've done to Green. Give me a stallion, a racer. I'll go and face Largol alone."

"We're coming with you," shouted Sammy.

"Try and stop us," cried Biddy, "after all we've been through together!"

Garret didn't argue but turned again to the king. "I'll take them some of the way. They'll need a carriage and some chargers."

"And a driver!" added Dartradisadene, bowing before the king. "For which, with Your Majesty's permission, I offer my considerable services."

"Go then," said the king. "Take everything you need. Be swift but cautious. Tonight before midnight, I'll light the fire above here on Bunkleen Mount." Then with his eyes fixed firmly on Garret, he added. "Your job is to ensure the Salmon Girl sings her song. With luck you'll get there before Largol and have your business done before he can stop you."

Within minutes they were galloping away, Garret leading the way on a gleaming steed that was so muscular and full with rearing enthusiasm that he found it difficult to restrain him, and the others rattling along behind in a two-pony carriage that was being driven at a demon's pace by Dartradisadene who was snapping his whip out in front and shouting, "*Yah! Yah! Yah!*"

Unknown to Garret was a disturbance on a trail parallel to the one that they were on, where a cluster of horsemen had broken away from the ranks of the trooping fairies to race for that place where another hidden passage led away from Bunkleen Mount and continued on to a rugged twisting path above ground that wound its way out into the dim distance of the night. Somewhere further on, this path, following a series of treacherous rises and dips and falls, would cross the one that he was on and then join it to traverse again further depths of the Great Northern Forest before, as one sinuous ledge, it went on to vein its way through the heights of the Winterlan Mountains, the downs of the Treefellwells Hills and the forested vale that led along the valley of the Greenback River and, lastly, to Linahen Rock and the seashore beyond.

Chapter 14

Once they had traversed the initial dark forested inclines and emerged on the outer path down from Bunkleen Mount, they took up speed again and pushed onwards with greater vigour and determination than would normally be afforded on such a darkened, twisted, and treacherous slope. Across the night, the forest was still and silent, a singular hush growing and spreading through the hulking ribs of the dark woods as if all the small night creatures that would have usually been foraging there had, for some reason, gone to ground. The moon was full and high with jagged ribbons of clouds chasing across its frozen yellow face, which in turn sent ghostly silver shadows wafting along the open ground and slipping in and out of the silhouettes of trees at the forest's edges in a sort of macabre dance.

They sped forward with no let up, until they reached another winding path that fell away from the hillside back into the forest. It was there where a sparse divide gave views across to the other side of the Great Northern Forest and its deep ravine that they first heard the thunder of hooves and the rumbling of wheels and spotted the hurried movement of a caravan's lights racing through the gloom. Garret guessed that it was Largol and his men, moving at greater speed than they were and, it seemed, on a wider and more direct road that lay on the other side of the forest, but he said nothing to the others. Although never one to give up, he could see no possible way that they could reach Linahen Rock before the speeding caravan, barring some unlikely mishap that would cause it to come to a halt. Dartradisadene, too, suspected that the trundle on the other side of the forest and the jumping lights there was Largol and a posse of his ruffians but also said nothing. Before anything, he was more concerned just then with keeping their carriage — that on several occasions had already been too close to going over the edges of the perilous slopes for comfort — on track on the dark path, not to speak of his reputation as a driver, and it was taking all of his concentration to do this.

Biddy, her cats, and the children were pummelled and rolled, rocked sideways and upwards and pulled over and under on the undulating roadway but never complained. More than once, they had glanced the wild determination in Garret's eyes when he held his eager stallion back to allow them to catch up. There was something else in his eyes also that none of them spoke about but all recognized. It was as if there was an immeasurable fear weighing down on him, a worry of incalculable proportions.

Sammy was being knocked around as much as the others in the small carriage, but his mind was on other things. Looking at Dervla, who was sitting across from him, he began to remember back to when the fairies took her and how for a while it seemed as though she would never be returned to their family again. He remembered then how some of the older people in Creel had always said that all things happen for a reason, and also how he had ridiculed them behind their backs for saying this. Now he was having second thoughts. It seemed his sister's abduction had happened for a reason and was part of some greater plan, like a cog that started a giant wheel turning or a ripple that spawned a wave. She had been an instrument that had been used to awaken actions in others that may have otherwise remained dormant and forever unused. The actions he was thinking of were those of Biddy when she had been so quick to offer them help after Dervla was taken and again when she heard about Garret's fight with the Mawlingfer and put her own needs aside to come with them. Then there was Garret himself and his willingness to help, for without him, they would surely have never found the Salmon Girl or convinced her to sing her song. Biddy's cats, too, had played their part as guides and watchers and protectors and showed intelligence above that given to mere beasts. Even those of the fairy kingdom, although initially for selfish reasons, were contributors and helpers and some still had roles to play. Green had given his life, and now Dartradisadene was risking his. As for the other children, their actions were as great if not greater than those of the witch, the wizard, and all the others put together. Not only had they left their homes to come on the journey, but they had also given him support in a way that only children can. Like him, they knew that their world, Lissendel, would come to an end if the fish stopped swimming to its rivers and shores and its crops failed. Without the livelihood given by the sea, the rivers, and the land, the whole place would begin to waste away. He knew that Lissendelians would never serve under Largol without revolt, no matter what he promised, and many would die because of this. Most would probably move off the island to unmapped lands in the uncharted seas, and the ones that did stay to serve Largol would be as good as dead themselves anyway. Eventually, Lissendel would cease to exist. The only chance they had to rid themselves of the threat that was hanging over them was by the successful conclusion of the events that were waiting to happen. Whether the Salmon Girl would ever get to sing her song he did not know, but he prayed that she would. In Sammy's mind, an immense bleakness was on the horizon, a black cloud that was blotting out the future that should be there. More and more, it was becoming evident that something bigger was looming that would decide everything: a meeting of titans was gathering pace, the black wizard against the white one, Largol against Garret Dimple. Perhaps this was the real reason why everything happened as it had, he thought. The outcome of the clash would be anybody's guess and while, since having come to know Garret he would back him in a fight against anybody in the known world, there was no telling how powerful Largol was. He knew too, that Garret by his own admission was all the time growing weaker without his shadow.

"Look! Up ahead! There are horsemen blocking the road!" cried the voice of Dartradisadene, struggling to project his voice with the constant rolling and jaunting of the carriage on the uneven trail. Garret, however, had already spotted the cluster of blackly clad riders near the crossroads that led onto the wider paths. "Keep moving and stay calm," he answered, pushing his stallion more determinedly out in front.

"There must be twelve of them. What will we do? We'll never take them?"

Garret slowed then. "There are thirteen of them. One of them has slipped in behind those trees to the right. He's the one to watch."

"Thirteen? Even worse!"

"We'll take them."

Dartradisadene was unconvinced. "Yeah, right," he said in a low murmur that was never meant to reach Garret's ears, but did.

Somehow in the darkness Garret's eyes singled out Dartradisadene's with a look of defiance that for a second chilled the Amadawn to his bones. Then he shouted to him, "Slow down till I give the word! Then charge for all your worth!"

Dartradisadene was confused but mostly fearful. "We'll be on top of them in a minute!"

It was only when they reached that part of the path that gave views of its whole meandering stretch ahead that they saw in detail the cluster of riders who lay in wait for them. Some of the riders were rearing their horses while others were boldly starting a slow trot towards them with an ominous and calculated confidence.

"Charge now!" called Garret, wielding his flashing staff as he thundered out in front without a moment's delay.

"Yah! Yah! Yah!" roared Dartradisadene, snapping his whip out immediately as if relieved to be racing forward again.

The riders before them showed no fear but grouped together and began to charge forward towards them. Only at the last minute, when Garret had waded into them, his staff swinging and cutting, did they spread out and start to disperse. Even then, it was too late, for as they broke apart their frighten horses were pushed aside and hacked apart when the thundering carriage driven by Dartradisadene careered down the dark path and hurtled straight into them. Some of the riders were thrown from their horses as they reared in panic and bolted, while others engaged Garret with their knives and swords in a most terrible violent tussle. Every clash of knife and sword brought a resplendent glow to Garret's staff as it deflected the attackers' assaults and sent lightning flashes back at them. Even then, the burly riders were not easily fought off, and it was only after several more of them had been dealt deathly blows from Garret's staff that they finally relented and drew back off the path.

Looking out from one side of the bounding carriage, Sammy gulped. "Look! They've - they've no faces!"

"They have faces! They're wearing hoods," answered Biddy, looking out from the other side.

"No, really! They haven't!" shouted Sammy as the rider who Garret saw slipping into the trees suddenly came racing from behind them to scramble from his horse onto the back of the carriage. Immediately, there was uproar, as Dervla, Louise, and Maeve caught sight of the faceless attacker. Padraig thought to oust him before he could get a foothold but was himself pushed back and unbalanced by the velocity of the bounding and jolting carriage. Seeing this, Biddy and her cats, Penny and Pinch, started to take on the black intruder. A massive furore ensued then with wrestling and pushing and shouting and screaming before Biddy and her cats found themselves on their backsides in a ditch on the side of the road, a little bemused, but miraculously unscathed, having been thrown from the hurtling carriage by the brawny intruder.

"Take the reins! I'll deal with him!" bawled Dartradisadene to Sammy when he became aware of the commotion. Sammy though, was struggling to help Padraig back to his feet, while also trying to move Dervla, Louise, and Maeve out of harm's way. It was just as the intruder was preparing to launch another attack that a blaze and blow came in from one side of the carriage and knocked him off his feet. Dazed then as he tried to gather himself, he shuddered and scrambled away all at once as he became aware of the monstrous figure that was standing over him, threateningly. Suddenly, the children saw the figure too, and for a moment were equally as frightened as the intruder. Yet something was telling them *not to be afraid*. In the half-light of the bounding and trundling carriage, they all saw something familiar in the beast's eyes. It was Garret; his body lost in a terrifying form-change that made the intruder look timid, unimposing, and even diminutive by comparison. When Dartradisadene glanced back and saw the beast, he exclaimed. "It's the devil himself!" He wasn't to know that his cry was the distraction that caused Garret to look around for another intruder and that gave the one there his chance to get away. In the racing carriage, piebald with grey-light and darkness and flashes of red and green fierceness from Garret's eyes, all the children saw was the seemingly petrified, if faceless, intruder taking his chance to run when he really had no chance. They saw him leap from one terror into another, jump from a known fear into one unknown. Perhaps in his mind it was taking the easy way out - but as they watched his desperate leap from the speeding carriage into the dropping darkness of the gaping precipice off the twisted path, which surely had a jagged fall all the way down to an unforgiving bottom that was waiting there to break him - they knew that there was no easy way out. His fall was silent, a lone soul plummeting into an indefinite darkness leaving no sound to confirm what its fate had been.

By the time Dartradisadene had pulled the carriage to a halt, the children were watching in astonishment as Garret began to shrink back from the huge beastly proportions of his form-change to his own slender self. It all seemed to happen at once, too — his head, torso and legs coordinated in a singular scaling down until he was almost himself again. The last to change was the pallor of his face, which suddenly crunched and contorted from one that had been hairy and primal to that of the wizen old wizard. Minutes later, Biddy and her cats emerged through a cloud of dust that had been left by the carriage's abrupt stop to join the others who were all now gathered around Garret querying him about his form-change.

"We're okay!" said Biddy and when none of the others responded, she tried for their attention again. "No, really, we're okay!"

One by one, then the children began to breathe a sigh of relief that they had been spared from further attacks of the intruder by Garret's intervention (even though he, too, in his beastly form-change had initially frightened them more than the intruder).

"Penny and Pinch and I obviously frightened the intruder off then," boasted Biddy. "Lucky for him that we accidentally... ahem... fell out of the carriage when we did. He was fighting a losing battle, big and burly though he was. He was no match for us!"

"Garret saw him off," said Louise casually.

Biddy ignored this and began to stroke her cats affectionately. "He was no match for us. Isn't that right, my pets?"

Penny and Pinch both meowed as if in confirmation of this.

"When the intruder dumped you and your cats out of the carriage, Garret turned into a huge beast and saved us," enthused Dervla. "He was amazing!"

"You did your best, Biddy," Maeve said.

"But it just wasn't good enough!" sniggered Padraig.

Biddy was distraught. "He dumped us out of the carriage?"

"Afraid so, Biddy. And if it wasn't for Garret..." explained Sammy, before asking when he realized that Garret was nowhere to be seen, "Where is Garret?"

When the others looked to see where Garret had gone, they couldn't find him either, but then they heard the sound of his horse rearing up and galloping off down the winding road that lay ahead of them.

CHAPTER 15

After an hour of worried waiting in which Garret failed to return and the road that he had gone down had been devoured by a steel-grey mist, Biddy reasoned that he must have decided to go it alone against Largol after all. It was such a noble thing to do (but so in keeping with the good wizard's nature), she thought, to go out into the night on his own to face unknown terrors from such a horrible adversary. He would have been thinking of them when he left, worried for their safety, concerned about their welfare. And although Biddy knew that all the things that Garret did were unquestionably for the good of others and that the amount of sacrifices that he was always willing to make had no boundaries or limits, she still feared that this time his bold braveness and unmitigated selflessness may just lead to his downfall.

Without sharing her fears, she rallied the others together and prepared them to carry on. She knew it was too late to turn back, and anyway, it seemed, on those black desolate slopes that there was no other road or path that they could take that would present any less danger. She was waiting for some of the children to object to going on following the ordeal of the attack and was surprised when they didn't. Either she had underestimated their courage or they had just misjudged the gravity of the events that were still waiting to unfold. She went to check this with them too, but laughed when she poked her head into the carriage and found all of them suddenly asleep. Even her cats, Penny and Pinch, were there lost in sleep. Outside, Dartradisadene was busy readying the team of horses for the rest of the journey with comforting words like *steady* and *down* and *back*. It was when they began to move again that the combination of the rocking carriage and the passing nightscape, imageless in that place against its own yawning shroud, also caused Biddy to forget her fears and lulled her into the same infinite slumber as the others where she began to dream of her home.

In Dartradisadene's mind, much of what went before would occur again that night before they reached their journey's end. There was still a long way to go, a long road with treacherous twists and bends to negotiate and fallen boulders to avoid and shingled surfaces that would allow the carriage wheels little or no grip and that would cause them to slide. These natural dangers combined with the many overhanging and precipitous cliffs and falls that hugged the whole route were in themselves daunting, but added to the poor visibility in the misted darkness of that night, it gave him an uncomfortable sense of apprehension that he knew would stay with him until they reached their destination. Niggling his thoughts also was the fear that another ambush like the one they had fought off just then or one of an even more defiant and malicious nature was waiting to ensnare them somewhere further along the way. Absentmindedly, he played with the consideration that it had only been luck that saved them earlier, before realizing that it had nothing to do with luck but with the fierceness in battle of Garret, someone he feared even more than the threat of the uncertain roads and the likely mishaps that lay waiting on them. It was then that he began wishing that Garret hadn't gone off into the night leaving them to fend for themselves.

"Yah! Yah! Yah!" he shouted suddenly again, his eyes staring and glazed. "Charge you miserable creatures, or I'll whip the living daylights out of you! Charge, I said!" But even though the carriage increased its speed to an ungodly pace it was still not enough for him. Standing up he snapped the whip viciously across the horses' heads while holding on tightly to their reins. All the time, his demeanour seemed to be deteriorating into something gross and primal, his mind racing faster and faster with a terrifying energy that made him shout louder and louder the harder he worked the horses.

Now the road was coming at them quickly, too quickly, the twists and turns straightening out and descending so that the thundering carriage began to bound and jolt with its own velocity. Several times, they came near to going over the jagged fall off the side of the rugged path, the carriage skirting the very edge of the cliff and half straddling over it, only to skate back onto the path again in a shaky skid that spat up tangled plumes of black dust and stones. Laughing deliriously, Dartradisadene had no control over his actions. He was cocooned inside a deafening rush through a black hole that was ever widening as if to swallow them. He could hear himself laughing and shouting but was lost as to the reason why. Coming from behind, he could hear the screams and calls of the others begging him to slow down, but he couldn't slow down. It had been a long time since he had experienced such exhilaration, and although he knew that the faster they went on the treacherous path the more danger they would be exposed to, he couldn't help but push the carriage's team of horses for more and more speed.

Biddy was last to wake up in the trundling carriage but first to see that the maddened glaze in Dartradisadene's eyes was not his own doing but possible caused by a spell cast on that stretch of road earlier by Largol, as was the sleep (she now suspected) that had suddenly befallen all of them. Around her, the children were all in a panic, shouting and screaming, as they were being bustled and jolted from one side of the carriage to the other. Perhaps that was why she found herself outside the dashing carriage, moments later, and hanging on desperately as she edged along on a thin wooden seam to try to reach where Dartradisadene was.

"Stop, you fool! You Amadawn!" she shouted several times only to be ignored by the entranced driver. It was when she reached where he was and saw the full extent of his mesmerism that she gave up trying to get his attention. Now she concentrated her efforts on trying to pry the reins out of his grasp, pulling and dragging at them viciously, while making sure never to touch his hands for fear that she would be turned into an Amadawn too. Biddy's efforts, however, were all to no avail. Dartradisadene's hands (like his mind) were clenched in an unrelenting vice-grip that would take strength greater than that possessed by Biddy to open. She had resigned herself to this fact when, out of the blue, a rider appeared before them in the grey light at the bottom of the sloping road and, as if in defiance, reared his horse before advancing towards them. The carriage's momentum was lifting its wheels from the road and spinning them wildly before rasping them down again on the uneven incline. Even if the rider's horse had lightening speed he could not avoid being hit by the speeding carriage, thought Biddy, before being left utterly speechless when the rider dismounted and stood out in the road before them, his hands held high.

As they got nearer to where he was, Biddy tried one last time to wrench the reins from Dartradisadene's grip. It was a last effort that, even if it were only to stop the poor mindless wretch that was standing in the road before them from being run over and brutally squashed, would be worthwhile, but it was not to be. Again, the carriage vaulted over the undulating ground and in doing so jolted Biddy from the relative safety of where she had been to a desperate foothold that saw her grasping at a side handrail of the carriage just to hang on. With her grasp slipping and the velocity of the carriage ever increasing on the downward slope, it seemed that it would only be a matter of time before she would weaken and let go, and then fall to what would be a certain death.

"Wake up, Amadawn! Slow down beasts! You've fallen foul to a devious spell. Stop, I say!" said an echoing voice as a peel of thunder rolled across the sky and a flash of lightning shot to ground nearby.

"And not before your time!" whimpered Biddy jadedly regaining her foothold, as the carriage slowed to a halt within a whisker of where the rider, who she now realized was Garret Dimple, stood.

Dartradisadene was confused. "What...where...? What's happening? Where are we?"

"Wake up, Amadawn. There's still a fair way to travel," said Garret, climbing up onto the carriage and taking over the reins from Dartradisadene.

"I was in some tunnel," answered Dartradisadene, bemused. "At least, that's what it seemed like."

Sammy jumped from the carriage and protested to Garret. "He nearly drove us over the edge, the whole lot of us! Where were you, Garret? We might have all been—"

"Everyone's safe now," confirmed Garret. "That's all that matters, hey?"

Sammy went to protest once more. "Well yes, but—"

"Then we must continue!" interrupted the wizard. "We've no time to lose, and there are still some dangers to be tackled before we reach Linahen Rock."

"Don't ask how I am," said Biddy sarcastically to her cats who came curling around her feet, meowing. "I've only been punched senseless by some faceless attacker, dumped from a speeding carriage, put under some dizzy sleeping spell, battered, bruised, and then, while trying to bring that Amadawn to his senses, almost thrown off the carriage again. But don't ask how I am! I'm fine!"

The children in the carriage were still a little groggy and confused but still found time to giggle at Biddy's sarcasm.

When they began to move Garret gave the reins back to Dartradisadene and mounted his horse again but rode nearer to the carriage than before as if to give comfort to those inside. Dartradisadene was ready to race the carriage's team of horses again but stopped when Garret beckoned to him to go slowly, whispering, "If there's going to be another attack it'll be round the next bend at the overhanging valley. A few men could halt an army there. It's narrow and treacherous, so beware."

"But isn't that all the more reason I should charge the horses, so that they don't have a chance to attack us?"

Garret's eyes blazed. "I said that it's narrow and treacherous too. Charge the horses and you'll bring down the whole valley on top of us! It's a place of landslides, so hold the horses back, or we'll all be sorry!"

"Oh..." coughed the Amadawn, feeling ill at ease.

"Everyone out," called Garret then, his head angled though the carriage's window. "I'm sorry but this place is too dangerous to be caught sitting down; this carriage will offer you no protection if the rocks begin to fall like they're so prone to do in this cursed valley. So out now and walk behind! And you, Amadawn, lead the team on foot from the front."

As the night deepened, they began to trek through the treacherous pass that in some places stabbed upwards towards the sky with jagged peaks and in others arched back in on itself with precarious overhanging boulders that seemed balanced on a knife-edge. Against the enormity of the valley, they were a thin line of movement that was barely discernable on the black twisting road: Garret on foot, leading his horse, followed by Dartradisadene, his team of horses and the carriage and then Biddy, her cats, and the children. The slowness, caution, and silence with which they proceeded would have resulted in them never having been detected, had it not been for the flickering of the lantern on the side of the carriage.

When they had almost reached the halfway stage through the pass, their spirits were lifted momentarily when they saw the full moon again, now peach-coloured, moving from behind a bank of white-grey cloud, high on the horizon, its face fat with laughter. It lit the way ahead and seemed welcoming. Even the black cliffs on either side (that to the children had been ominous dark sentinels whose eyes had observed their every move) were no more than old rock-stacks with a mystery that had seemed fearsome in the darkness, but that in the glowing moonlight had a strange, if dissipated, beauty.

The light coming down on the valley even took Garret aback. Enthralled, he had almost forgotten not to make noise and would have shouted to the others about the moonlight on the valley being such a glorious sight, had he not remembered that the whole hillside might have come plummeting down on them with the least little sound. Even when he looked up and saw a dark figure in movement, a fleeting shape caught in silhouette against the backdrop of the skyline, he stopped himself from shouting a caution to the others or reacting in any way. For a moment, he had even convinced himself that it may have been a trick of the changing light, but soon realized that what he was seeing was real when another dark figure crossed his vision. Seconds after, a trickle of stones and dust, no bigger than that that would have been kicked up by a single footfall, came from an overhanging ledge to spray the road in front of them. It was enough though to alarm Garret and to cause him to raise a hand to the others to bring them to a halt. Then he waited, listening for another fall or some sound that would further confirm that he was right to be cautious about going forward. The rolling thunder that followed was more than he expected and in that instant understood, for his initial reaction was to freeze for a split second that, in his mind, lasted an eternity. The others, too, just stood there blankly looking at one another as if with disbelief. Slowly, the realization came over Garret that a landslide was happening directly above them, not in front or behind but right where they were at that very moment, and that their only escape was to move forward as quickly as possible. Suddenly, and as if by instinct, Dartradisadene's team of horses raced away with the carriage past Garret, causing him to jump to one side and in doing so to come to his senses.

"Run!" he shouted to the others. "Run now! This way!"

Already, Dartradisadene was in pursuit of the runaway carriage, his scurry turning quickly into a spinning whirlwind that threw out clouds of dust as he cut through a small cascade of falling debris from the ever-increasing landslide. Biddy and the children moved quickly when they heard the call but had it not been for Garret who, mounted on his horse, returned to where they were to whisk them to safety, they would have surely come to an end that none of them would wish to dwell upon or ponder, for only seconds were to pass before the first terrifying avalanche came down. Garret's bravery, lightening speed, and articulate horsemanship in managing his frightened stallion under threat of the thundering landslide were the things that saved them. Again and again, he negotiated a path through the rain of rock and rubble to work his way towards them, snatching Maeve, Louise, and Dervla onto the broad back of his horse on his first run, Padraig and Sammy on his second, and then Biddy on his third. Indeed, he had planned, even amidst the mad confusion of the landslide, to take Biddy's two cats, Penny and Pinch, on the third run with her, but they were nowhere to be seen.

At the height of the landslide there was a great explosion from above. It seemed that the whole hillside was sliding down and that the very earth that they stood on was about to crack open and swallow them. Dartradisadene had successfully recovered the carriage, backed it up, and was anxiously waiting for the others to come. Garret, however, was playing with the thought of going back once more to try to find Biddy's cats, but the rock-fall that followed was of such a massive intensity that it made going back near impossible, even for the wizard.

"No! No!" wept Biddy, not wanting to accept what seemed inevitable. "Not my pets! Not my beauties!"

Garret felt helpless as he looked at the dusty black deluge coming down on the road where they had been. "We have to move on. It's too dangerous here."

The children then rushed to the carriage and started to climb on board, the three girls breathlessly scrambling on first, followed by Padraig and Sammy, who were stopped before they got on by Dervla, who emerged from the carriage shouting. "Biddy! Biddy! Penny and Pinch are here in the carriage! Come and see for yourself!"

Almost in disbelief, Biddy ran forward. She was already wondering why Penny and Pinch (who must have slipped back into the carriage without her knowledge) hadn't run out to greet her having been through such an ordeal as that of the landslide. However, she didn't have to wonder for long, because when she stepped up into the carriage, she saw that they were soundly asleep and had most likely been there that way throughout the whole horrible downpour. Even when they woke, they seemed at a loss as to why everyone was looking at them with such incredulous expressions on their faces and as to why Biddy was giving them so many extra hugs and kisses.

Finally, they began moving again. The road seemed less treacherous from then on, but Garret, as vigilant as ever, never ceased watching the remaining slopes off either side of the road as he led the way ahead.

CHAPTER 16

Thirty minutes later, when the road dipped through a forested vale and emerged onto a great winding plateau of the Treefellwells Hills where it fell away into a tree-lined valley, they caught their first sight of the meandering waters of the Greenback River and further on the coastline. The moon was slowly moving westward now; its silvery glow making white streaks on the river's eddies and beyond this white crests on the waves of the dark sea as it came ashore.

Bringing them to a halt, Garret looked back through the darkness but could barely see the treacherous path that they had travelled such were its undulations and twists and turns. Still visible though through the murk of the night valley was the deepening purple shadow of Bunkleen Mount, its massive rise looking immovable against the sky. Although distant and dark, the more Garret peered at it the more detail he saw. At first, there were just odd orange sparks, briefly glowing before disappearing. Then, when he thought his eyes had failed him, there appeared a full bracelet of light that went from the base of the immense mount to its very pinnacle, where minutes later to his utter joy and amazement, a fire began to grow.

The children watched the glow from the growing fire in wonderment too. Coming down the valley, it had an almost magical quintessence, as if there was more to it that just the burning of wood.

"King Lugh's kept his promise," said Sammy, as Garret called for them to move on again.

Dervla was apprehensive. "But what happens now?"

"Now Garret has to face his foe," answered Biddy. "And if he fails to get the better of him, we may all look out."

Louise reacted immediately. "What if Largol gets the better of him?"

"He won't," snapped Padraig, before turning to Biddy, and muttering less than convincingly, "He...he won't..."

"All our journeying will have been for nothing," said Maeve, before reconsidering and saying, "I mean...well, at least we freed Dervla, and that's something."

Sammy was quick to show his support for Garret. "Garret won't let us down. He hasn't let us down once. And he knows that it's not just us who are depending on him, but the whole of Lissendel."

"Yes, but without his shadow?" cautioned Biddy.

"Biddy, could you not make up a spell that would help Garret against Largol?" asked Louise.

Biddy laughed weakly (and wishfully) at the thought. "I don't have that sort of power. My spells are really just old remedies and concoctions that have certain beneficial effects but no real clout, and they have nowhere near the power needed to do what you're asking. I'm afraid Garret will have to face Largol on his own. Then again, he'll tell you himself that that's the way he'd prefer it."

From there, the descent to the seashore was easy. They moved slowly in and out of broken forest in an almost hallowed silence that was breached only by the clip-clop of the their horses' hooves and the tender wash of the tide on the seashore as they neared the lower run of land that led to Linahen Rock. By the angle of the moon's position in the sky and its distance from the horizon, Garret worked out that there was still some hours to go till midnight. All of them had feared that there would be a final attack set up by Largol and his men before they reached Linahen Rock, and although there was no indication that one would happen, they moved stealthily all the way down as if expecting this fear to be realized.

Linahen Rock and the nearby hillside were shrouded in silence when Garret eased his horse out into the opening and sidestepped it down the slant that led to its base. He had already waved Dartradisadene and the others away, knowing that it would be safer for them to stay back until he could assess what lay in wait for them and baring in mind the sacrifice that would come due when and if Aoife sang her song. He had expected that Largol and his men would have set up an encampment there but was surprised when all he saw was the hunched figure of a darkly clad man sitting alone before a small open fire. Dartradisadene and the others, who had made their way up onto the hillside overlooking Linahen Rock, were surprised also, when they saw no sign of an encampment or any men other than the one sitting before the fire.

When Garret proceeded down to where he was, the man never once looked up from the fire, even when he got so near that it became virtually impossible for him to be unaware of his presence there. His rugged face and pensive eyes, hooded and barely visible, gave nothing away as to his identity but clearly portrayed his mood. He seemed preoccupied by another concern. It was as if his eyes were trying to find an answer to some dilemma in the dancing flames of the fire. Even when he lifted a saucepan and poured a steaming dark liquid into a cup and drank from it, he seemed totally oblivious to Garret. Garret, nevertheless, knew to be on his guard. If it was Largol, he thought, his apparent lack of concern and even unreadiness would have only been a ploy, a calculated and devious ruse that would have been designed to draw him in.

"Tea?" offered the man finally, his coarse but somehow sophisticated voice, breaking the sound of Garret dismounting and tying up his horse.

"Is that what it is?" came Garret's reply, sampling the pungent aroma in the air.

"Yes. Only tea, I'm afraid."

"Smells nice, but I don't want any just now."

"So what do you want then?"

Garret said nothing for a moment but looked around suspiciously, as if expecting someone else to be there. Then he asked, "Who are you?"

"Sit down, why don't you?" answered the man.

As if to get a clearer look at the man, Garret crossed to the other side of the fire and sat down directly opposite him. Still the man kept his head down, his hood making a shadow across his face. It was when Garret swept his own cloak back across his shoulder and this caused some sparks to fly wildly from the fire that the man looked up for moments that were long enough to reveal the detail of his face. It was a forceful but boldly handsome face with high cheeks that were crisscrossed with lines of laughter or anger and framed by square rugged jawbones.

"Are you Largol Despalt?" asked Garret, even though he instinctively knew the answer before it was confirmed when Largol looked up and smiled.

"And you're the great Garret Dimple! Here to fight with me, are you?"

"If that's what it takes."

"All these years and we've never once met up. People even have us down as sworn enemies. If we were friends, we'd have lots to talk about now, you know."

"We still have lots to talk about."

"But if I'm not mistaken, you've come here without your shadow...to pick a fight. Now you're a brave one, I'll say that. You'd have some chance against me with the backup of your shadow behind and before you, but none without it. So why don't you just go home? Have some tea before you go, why don't you."

Garret's eyes flared keenly. "If you're so confident of my having 'no chance' against you without my shadow, why send your men to ambush us on the road? To me, it sounds like you were afraid to face me yourself!"

"I'm facing you now, aren't I?" grinned Largol spitefully, before glancing up at the hillside where all the others were. "Oh... and where are your little friends? Have they fallen by the wayside or are they just sneaking about somewhere out of sight?"

"Where are your blackguards?" retaliated Garret.

Largol paused for a moment, his eyes brightening with satisfaction as he sipped his tea. Garret found himself experiencing a very strong temptation to take some tea too, as its ever-manipulating aroma wafted around where they sat.

"My lads are out and about doing my business, if you must know," answered Largol finally, before standing up to look back across the valley. "Oh look! King Lugh is lighting a fire on top of Bunkleen Mount! Is he feeling the cold do you think, or is it some sort of signal? Perhaps it's a signal for the Salmon Girl to sing her song?"

"Something like that."

"This place is changing, Garret," warned Largol then. "The things that we hold on to really hold on to us and drag us down. Old ways block new ones, traditions stop us progressing, and when we stop going forward, we stagnate and die. That's the thinking of these times, man. Soon there will be no place in the world for special ones such as you and me. You must know that, Garret. You must feel that our days are numbered, hey?"

"Are we that special?"

Largol's laughter came and went in an instant of derision. "Of course," he said, "as far as you're concerned every miserable creature that walks the highways and byways of Lissendel is special."

"That's right."

As if he could sense Garret's weakening resistance to the aroma of the tea and his longing to taste it, Largol refilled his own cup and then poured one for Garret and placed it before him. "You're wrong, you know," he started again. "There are leaders and followers, rulers and those they preside over. It's always been that way. It's a like a permanent fixture in the lives and minds of everyone down the ages, a game that you and I take part in but never realize. A game that, because of our special powers, we control. We must control it. You see its continuance is down to us. It feeds off us and we in turn are fed by it. It's our responsibility. There is no choice. If the game ends, so do we. We will be forgotten. So why not join with me, Garret? Together we could perform endless wonders for the game! We could live like the most magnificent princes ever to grace these lands! Lissendel is just a poor imitation of what it could be with us leading the way! Can you not see this, man?"

"Your mind's not your own, Mister. It's been twisted by all the badness that you've nurtured down the years and warped by your own black deeds," answered Garret, trying to keep his mind from drifting into the ever-welcoming stupor that was ghosting around him tantalisingly, and that was caused by the fragrance from the tea. "If my end has to come, and it comes eventually for all of us, then let it be. And I would rather be forgotten altogether than remembered for the wrong reasons. I could never join with the likes of you for any glory or any cause. You're a madman and a menace!"

"You disappoint me, Garret Dimple. What is it that you want?"

Garret looked at him sternly. "I want the fish to swim again to Lissendel's shores and to her rivers. I want the threat on her lands lifted. I want you to return to your own place and to stop your meddling in these parts. I want you to lift whatever black spell it is that you've placed on us. Go home, man!"

"But the fish will come again! The rivers will be overflowing with them. There will be new crops, giant crops, the likes of which have never been seen before!"

"All this when you rule?"

"It's not such a bad thought, is it? And with the great Garret Dimple by my side there would be no boundaries to what we could achieve!"

"So I'm the great Garret Dimple again, am I?" quipped Garret sarcastically.

Largol reacted stoutly. "Lissendel has to grow strong! It must! Already wayward outsiders, who are full of self-interest and who have no understanding of or respect for the old ways, have infiltrated our towns and villages. As you know, the *Mawlingfer Shadowtakers* have been here already, and more will come. They're greedy. They've been spying on us and drawing up plans to invade us. One day their armies will be on our doorsteps. You've even been a victim of theirs! What chance have the ordinary folk got? What will happen when they come to take Lissendel from us, if we're weak and unprepared?"

"They'll be dealt with in time!" snapped Garret angrily. "Right now, I'm here to deal with you! And are you not also full of self-interest, too? "

"My interest is in keeping Lissendel under Lissendelian rule. You and I have the power to make that happen. With me, you will be more powerful than you could ever imagine. Together we could repel even the greatest armies. No one would dare come against us!"

"Our minds differ and so do our works. Mine will always oppose yours because you can't see the evil that you do, and I see nothing else! The threat of an invasion by the Mawlingfer beasts is convenient for you, is it not? I feel that there's someone powerful behind them, distorting their minds. Perhaps someone like you, Largol Despalt!"

A tense moment of silence ensued.

"You won't ever join up with me, will you?" said Largol then, his voice almost waning. "And it would seem that I either lift my spell or that I'm going to have a raging battle with you on my hands."

Now Garret was beginning to feel that Largol really wanted to avoid a fight with him. "That's right," he retorted. "The choice is yours!"

In another tense moment, Largol stood up and walked a short distance away, and then he returned to where Garret was and sat down again, smiling submissively at him. "You were right you know, when you said that I didn't want to face you. Not that I believe for one moment that I couldn't take you without your shadow, but one never really knows how the cards will fall when the likes of us do battle, and I never like to leave such things to chance."

"So you'll lift the spell?" asked Garret.

"I'm afraid it's too late for that," answered Largol, but when he saw Garret stirring and making for his staff, he added quickly, "So we'll just have to let the Salmon Girl sing her song. That was your original idea, and it should do the job!"

Garret's temper calmed a little then, but he was still suspicious. "If you're trying to trick me," he said, "I promise I'll make you pay."

"It's over," answered Largol. "The Salmon Girl is free to sing her song whenever she wants. So the fish will swim again, and the crops will grow too, but you'll still have to deal with the *Mawlingfer Shadowtakers* when they come in force. I'll fulfil my dreams of ruling Lissendel someday, one way or the other. It's a pity though, that you won't be around to share it with me."

"Lissendel's the home of many a good man and they'll rise up if they're threatened. Of that, I'm sure."

"I think they'll run into the ground like frightened mice, because they're weak and have no leadership!" retorted Largol then, before raising his cup acceptingly. "But for now join me in a toast to their future, even if it is only tea that we drink? To the Salmon Girl and her song and to the future of Lissendel!"

Garret hesitated for a moment but then picked up his cup and tapped Largol's with it in recognition of his toast. But when they drank and he saw the black wizard smiling deviously, his own face grew dim with a grimace for it was becoming obvious that something was amiss.

From above, Biddy and the others were straining in their efforts to try to see what was happening. To Biddy, the pleasantly captivating aroma that was wafting up from the steaming pot of dark liquid before where the two wizards sat was strangely familiar. Although she was at a loss as to the exact content and mixture of herbs and plants that she was almost sure had been used in its preparation, she knew in one terrifying instant of realization, that it was not a tea at all but a most potent and deadly poison. In panic, she worked out what it meant but realized - when she rose breathlessly and began to shout down to Garret not to drink the noxious black tea - that it was already too late. Then, with the others coming around her to see what was wrong, she sighed helplessly as if all her breath had been taken, saying, "No! No! No!" Finally, her voice stuttered into a silence that the others knew not to question, for standing now they could see everything that she could. Below in the glow of the fire one wizard was still sitting while the other had keeled over. It didn't take them long to work out that the one who had fallen was Garret Dimple.

"Is Garret...is he...?" Sammy attempted to ask the question that none of them really wanted an answer to (*was Garret dead?*), but he was unable to get the words out.

"He can't be...dead, can he?" cried Louise.

Dervla answered quickly, her voice filled with desperation. "No! No!"

"This is all my fault, isn't it?" said Dervla.

"Don't die on us now, Garret Dimple! Don't die on us now!" shouted Padraig in his loudest voice, and his troubled call caused an echo to repeat several times across the valley to make it seem that all the mountains were making the same plea.

Biddy said nothing for a while. Through the darkness, her eyes were searching for some signs of life in Garret's face, and, while the distance made it difficult to distinguish any detail, for a split second she thought that she had seen him smile. However, it didn't take her long to dismiss this as a trick of the light and of her own inability to accept that he had truly gone and to sink swiftly into an indolence that was caused by her grief. Quickly though, her grief was stunted by a new feeling of fear when her cats, Penny and Pinch, both sniffed the air and arched their backs with snarling alertness, and she became aware of a creeping sensation all around. Too late, the children sensed the danger and then noticed the leering figures that were skulking in the shadows. As was the case with Biddy, there was no time for them to react before the dark villains broke out from their hides and were on top of them, trapping their efforts to escape and tackling their every run until they were all tied up and being led down to where Largol waited. Only Dartradisadene, who had been off to a sheltered side when the assault came, was able to escape, turning himself into a menacing dust devil that thwarted the efforts of the attackers to capture him and allowed him to slip away into some nearby trees where he waited to see what would unfold.

CHAPTER 17

When Largol called the rest of his men from the surrounding woods, they dropped out of the branches of the trees and climbed out of shallow leaf-covered hides beneath the soil. By then, Biddy and children had been caged in the very carriage that brought them there, their hands and legs secured from side to side with ropes that made movement virtually impossible. Even Biddy's cats were bound in such a way that escape or movement was out of the question. In another carriage driven forward by a hairy stump of a beast that responded to Largol's calls with horrifying guttural cries, there were several transparent spheres with small wriggling figures inside of them who were fighting to break free. One of the small figures was that of a red-haired leprechaun, his fists bleeding from his efforts to escape, another was a hooded figure of diminutive man with no face that could be seen but with eyes that shone with fiendish intent, and yet another, the tiny shimmering figure of a silver-winged girl, her sallow face tracked with tears.

Crouched behind a thick clump of bushes nearby, Dartradisadene waited and watched it all. He was totally undecided as to what action to take. In his mind, every possible circumstance that he could imagine — and he strained himself to think of every one that would bring a favourable solution to the dilemma facing them — led only to the same dim conclusion that he dared not ponder, lest it would become reality. Yet, at that moment, it seemed the future of Lissendel was in Largol's hands and his alone. What was he to do? From where he watched, it seemed that all was lost. Garret was slumped listlessly beside the fire, the carriage where Biddy and children were imprisoned was surrounded by guards, and Largol, standing unchallenged on a mound before Linahen Rock, was issuing new instructions to another grisly band of his ruffians. In the distance across the valley, he could see the dancing glow of the fire on Bunkleen Mount. Now he began to think that if he could somehow get word to King Lugh of how badly everything had worked out and of how desperate they were for help, the old king would surely send them some. But then he realized that it was already too late, and that even if he could contact the old king, his help would never arrive in time to be of any use to them. Midnight was looming, and it seemed that the whole future of Lissendel was in the balance and dependent on his next actions, ones that he was uncertain of and afraid to make.

It was when Largol began to send his men into hiding again, and it became obvious that he was setting a trap there for the Salmon Girl that Dartradisadene suddenly knew what he had to do. He had to warn her before she got there and remembering Green's dying words to King Lugh about how *she would come ashore before midnight near Linahen Rock*, if possible before she even emerged from the sea. Once on land, she would be at Largol's mercy, and while he knew that she must sing her song at midnight that night, it just might be possible that she could do this at that very time but from another safer place. With no time to lose he dashed out from the undergrowth, skipping and bounding down a slope and through another lower clump of trees that brought his stride to a momentary halt and caused him to redirect his run. His new route was no easier though, and it was only some minutes after, when the terrain got bumpier and narrower, that he went sliding over a sharp hillock and tumbled down on all fours. Luckily, his movement, lost against those of Largol's ruffians who were all around, went unnoticed. Immersed in his rush through the darkness to get to the seashore, he was almost oblivious to them and to the danger they presented. All he could think of was to get to Aoife and to warn her of the trap that lay waiting for her before she emerged from the night sea. After minutes, he began to hear the wash of the tide coming ashore and to smell its pungent aroma. He knew now that once he got over the next grassy hill that lay before him that this would lead down onto the sand dunes that circled that stretch of the coast and gave perfect views of the sea.

In a final breathless scurry, he dashed over the grassy hill and down to the seashore, stopping only once to make sure none of Largol's men had reached there before him. A cold breeze pushed at his face giving him welcome respite from his frantic run and allowing him to catch his breath before he started again. It was dark and empty on the seashore. Even though he was in the midst of a terrible panic, he couldn't help but admire the silken beauty of the high yellow moon reflecting on the purple sea where great waves were tumbled and reduced to whitewashed ribbons that broke in along the darkness of the shore. Its raw splendour for a moment stunted his movement and at the same time gave him a tremendous feeling of exhilaration. This was indeed something worth fighting for, he thought, and it somehow gave him the strength to go on. He ran on and on until he reached a place where a lone rock stood out from the sands. There was no sight or sound of anyone there, but something made him stop. Suddenly, he became aware of a peculiar and unsettling calmness that was all around that place. The breeze that had been so biting just minutes before was no longer there, and even the sound of the sea coming in seemed to have been hushed. In the silence, he could hear himself breathing. It was as if everything had been quietened in anticipation of some fantastic happening. Not long after then, there was a sudden rush and a flurry of movement of some small birds from a nearby sand dune that made him turn around with a gasp of expectation that he would see someone there, but there was no one. And yet he could still feel something was happening and someone was coming, and it was when he turned towards the sea again and a glistening creature broke the surface of the water and stood upright that these expectations were finally satisfied. Moments after the white misty figure of a beautiful girl emerged dripping from the tide and ghosted her way past where he was, as if oblivious to him. It was Aoife, the Salmon Girl, her haunting beauty binding his mind so much so that he almost forgot that he had come to warn her of the danger waiting at Linahen Rock.

"No!" he shouted finally. "No, Miss, Aoife! Don't go there. I beg you! Don't go to Linahen Rock!"

"Who are you, little one?" asked Aoife tenderly and without judgment.

"I'm King Lugh's Amadawn. Dartradisadene's my name."

"I see he's let the girl go and lit the fire on Bunkleen Mount to let me know. Now I have to keep my part of the bargain and sing my song at Linahen Rock."

"You can't!" protested Dartradisadene. "I mean, you mustn't go to Linahen Rock. Largol's waiting there for you. He's set a trap. He's captured the girl, Dervla, that King Lugh released, and he's imprisoned her brother and all her friends, too."

"And Garret Dimple?"

"I'm afraid he no longer with us. Largol tricked him into drinking a terrible poison."

Aoife could hardly talk such was her dismay. "Garret Dimple is..."

"The last I saw of him he was dead or dying without doubt," acknowledged Dartradisadene before warning, "So keep away from Linahen Rock, Miss. Sing your magic song from another place, or I fear you'll not get to sing it at all."

"But my song must be sung from there. It's as much about the magic of Linahen Rock as it is about my song. One part of the magic is nothing without the other. The fish will only swim if everything is done right. We've got no choice."

"But Largol and his men are there waiting for you!"

"Then we'll need some help," answered Aoife, picking up a white seashell and blowing into it.

Dartradisadene was puzzled and somewhat confused. He was at a loss as to what it was that Aoife was doing until a hollow whirring sound came from the seashell and filled the air to be answered from far off by what seemed to be its own echo. Looking out to sea with her eyes searching the whole length of its black horizon, it was as if she had called to someone and was waiting for them to come. Dartradisadene too, without knowing why, began to expect someone to come, but when no one did, he decided to ask what it was she was waiting for. He had hardly composed his question when a vast stirring occurred from the depths of the sea, which suddenly began to spit and bubble in a frightening and terrible rage. Then there was an ungodly yawning roar of many voices going up and the grinding sound of a gigantic chasm opening and closing, after which a huge crushing wash came ashore and crashed down onto the beachfront. When it retreated a brawny band of well-armed, scaly, man-like creatures were left in its wake that, at Aoife's beckoning, marched up the beach to join them.

"Friends of mine. Call them sea warriors," explained Aoife. "Now can we go to Linahen Rock?"

"Why, yes, of course," answered a suddenly amazed and delighted Dartradisadene, smiling proudly as he followed Aoife when she led them inland.

They had marched only a short distance when the moon's light playing across the grey darkness of the sands revealed some darker shapes moving against the humped rims of its dunes. This brought them to an abrupt standstill, which was almost an anticlimax, until from somewhere out of sight a strong voice called, "*Now!*" The seconds after fled in confusion in Dartradisadene's mind before he suddenly realized that Largol's men were swiftly attacking them from all sides and that there seemed to be no escape. With equal haste Aoife's sea warriors broke forward and engaged the dark attackers. Everywhere in the blackness, there were cries and calls and shouts, and the sounds of steel clashing against steel. Across the calamity, Dartradisadene's eyes found Aoife's. She was encircled by a defensive group of sea warriors who were fighting off every assault made by the dark attackers. The battle went on for some time with no ground won or lost by either side until there was an explosion that broke open the sea warriors circle and let the dark attackers in.

Dartradisadene, suddenly without regard for his own safety when he saw the fear in Aoife's eyes as Largol's men advanced on her, raced into a rage and spun himself into a violent wind that swirled up and down and gusted from side to side like a woodcutter's jagged blade. When the attackers were almost bearing down on Aoife, the insidious wind that he had become smashed through their ranks and tore them apart, leaving at least ten of them broken and limping away. Others dashed for cover but even some of these were too late to escape the violence and destruction that was meted out by the little Amadawn's terrible gusts. Only Aoife and her sea warriors were spared as the minute black storm that had surprised her as much as the attackers brought more destruction on the retreating assailants. Yet still, calls went up from some of them to renew their assault, but with the confusion and disarray caused by Dartradisadene's winds and the time it afforded the sea warriors to regroup, most of them just ran away. In another moment, the wind that had been so virulent just a short time before calmed to a gentle carpet of air that spoke to Aoife to reassure her that all was well before it lifted her away to a safe place. Although Aoife had heard much about the fairy wind, it was the first time she had ever seen it in action, and while she was most thankful for the help that it had given her, she was glad when it went away and Dartradisadene became himself again.

"That was fantastic!" enthused Aoife as she kissed the Amadawn's forehead. "You're my little saviour and my champion!"

Dartradisadene was preoccupied however, and somewhat embarrassed. "Yes, yes! But it's not over yet! Let's go to Linahen Rock now before it's too late!"

Without delay they clambered off into the darkness, Aoife bringing a halt to Dartradisadene's lead when he was opting to return to Linahen Rock on the same path that he had used earlier, saying that there was a quicker way to get there. Quicker it was, too, for it seemed only minutes after they had set out on the rugged and unfamiliar path through the darkness that they arrived at the sparsely forested outcrop of land that led up towards Linahen Rock. Yet such was their alertness following the attack that their senses rose to a perilous heightened peak where they began to play tricks on them, causing imagined movement all around, their eyes glimpsing distorted faces in the shadows and their ears hearing strange muffled noises and cries of suffering and desolation.

"W-We should have gone the other way!" said Dartradis-adene when an owl broke into flight from a nearby tree, causing him to jump back.

For a moment Aoife wanted to laugh at the look of sheer fright on the Amadawan's face but resisted the temptation to do this, saying softly and supportively, "We're almost there now."

Cautiously, they went down, Dartradisadene looking back for the sea warriors who were nowhere to be seen. "Where have the others gone, your sea warriors?"

"They'll come," she explained. "When the time is right, they'll come."

"But is this not the right time?"

"Apparently not," answered Aoife while she inwardly shared his concern as to why they had not followed them.

When they finally reached Linahen Rock, Aoife sighed sadly when she saw Garret's body slumped facedown near the fire. "Oh my poor, poor Garret Dimple...My poor, poor friend," she wept sadly. 'My love, Andale, was the song's first sacrifice and now it seems that you are its second. I'm sorry, so sorry my dear friend. But I promise you this, and I know that somehow you'll hear these words: nothing will stop me singing the song now. Nothing in heaven or on earth will stop me this night!"

"Hurry now, Miss Aoife," said Dartradisadene. "It must be near time now to sing your song!"

"But it's not quite midnight just yet," came a jeering voice from behind.

CHAPTER 18

Immediately and with some panic, they looked around to find themselves faced by Largol and some fifty of his ruffians who began to spread out around where they were, jeering and taunting them.

Dartradisadene pushed himself forward hesitantly. "You better back off now, Mister, or I'll, I'll..."

"Or you'll do what?" gloated Largol. "Turn into a little dust storm, the famous fairy wind?" Then raising his staff to the sky, he shot a crimson lightning bolt into a bank of unpretentious milky night-clouds that had been calmly drifting in from the sea, causing them to merge and mix together and to change colour into a murky black vapour that began to swell-up, spew out, and spin. In only minutes, the malignant mixture became a vile consuming monstrosity that, at Largol's command, began blowing everything askance and sucking up all in its path, while still bearing down with most of its might on a group of sea warriors who had been on their way to help, sweeping them off their feet and unceremoniously casting them here and there.

"The pathetic little gust that you become is no match for my tempest now, is it?" snarled Largol, tauntingly. "Look at how it makes your friends, the sea warriors, fly!"

Dartradisadene was suddenly fearless. "I'll still fight you," he said, gathering himself and spinning into a thunderous dust devil before going forward to attack. He was determined to strike the wizard with every ounce of strength in every coil of the winds that he could muster but was all at once taken aback when to his surprise, following a casual snap of Largol's fingers, he found himself bouncing off to one side and tumbling to a stop as if all his power had somehow been drained away.

"Go away little man!" laughed Largol. "You're beginning to bore me!"

In the sky above, Largol's now deafening storm was bulging into a grotesque shape that was quickly developing the characteristics of a gargantuan muscular body with a demonic sneering face, while rotating still with ever increasing velocity. It was lurching portentously over the whole place and seemed ready to come down to wreak havoc, when a blue streak shot out from somewhere behind where Largol stood and split through its heart with an immense flash that made it glow whiter that white. Aoife had fallen with the fright of it all, and Dartradisadene was cowering off to one side as if expecting another assault from Largol or one from his storm. Largol though, seemed strangely disconcerted. The look on his face was one of surprise, and his eyes betrayed the fact that for once he just didn't know what was happening. Only when the great light from the monstrous cloud had died down and his own shadow fell before him again in the sinking brightness, did he begin to work out what was happening and then start to feel another presence nearby. Who it was came to him in an instant, but he denied it, before considering that the blue shot that went up from behind to burst through his cloud just moments before, came from the same prowling presence that was next to him then and whose shadow should lie beside his, unless it had no shadow, unless it was Garret Dimple! When he turned and his fears were realized, he could only mutter. "You're...you can't be..."

"I never drank your poison," said Garret. "Did you really expect me to believe that you'd just give up and walk away, when I know you're the prince of lies?"

Largol's reaction was swift and venomous, pushing his cape open and swinging his staff around to fire a brace of lightning bolts at Garret who had to dive desperately for cover to avoid being hit, while also swinging his own staff upwards vigorously to create a shield to deflect them. Almost instantly, there was another volley of shots from Largol, then another and another. Although breathless and hunched low, Garret was still able to ward off the shots with blocking ones of his own that not only shielded him from the flashing bursts of Largol's lightning bolts but directed them back at the raging wizard causing him to duck for cover too.

At the edges of the nearby woods a group of sea-warriors who were recovering following the onslaught of Largol's storm were facing a new assault from Largol's ruffians.

"You can't stop me! No one can!" boasted Largol with a maddening roar, as he redoubled the amount and volatility of the shots from his staff that he was directing at Garret. "A wizard is nothing without his shadow! You're nothing!"

Still Garret was defiant. As if to dare and cajole Largol, he created a bigger target of himself for him by standing up and putting his own staff down. Largol was unperturbed at first and went on firing but quickly lost patience when his fire seemed incapable of finding its target. With simple unannounced movements, Garret played a game of chance with the black wizard whereby he merely dropped a shoulder, sidestepped, ducked, or jumped to avoid his incoming fire before daring him to try again. Not long after, however, Garret, beginning to tire, picked up his staff and once again used it as a shield. Each time Largol shot at him, he deflected it with a shot of his own and then returned another only to have it deflected too. An impasse ensued then that saw both of them shooting high and low and fast and slow in their efforts to hit each other with neither one succeeding. Their efforts would have been truly fruitless had it not been for the unannounced conception of a strange white light, bewildering to both of them, which began to glow in the place where the lightning fire from both of their staffs met and fused. It was a curious flitting illumination at first where Largol's red bolts and Garret's blue ones came together in one singular spot as if to test each other's strength, both with an energy that was unbending and irresistible. It was a white heat that sucked its power from both sources, a new gaseous force that, as it grew, would not be contained but spat and jumped out in all directions with volatile intensity and fabulous extremes of colour. One moment it rose as a burning white orb that rolled and pulsated, and the next, it swooped low and skimmed along the ground where it expelled erratic white bolts that shot outwards unpredictably. Neither of the wizards had experienced such power before, and both suddenly realized that they really could no longer control or contain it, for it seemed to have an intelligent will and fascinating power all of its own. Again, the orb rolled and rose and fell, but this time it bounced askew and ran off to one side in a most uncontrolled and wildly capricious way. It was as if some internal wrestling was taking place that would not be contained until it came apart. Seconds after, it did.

The great white light that filled the orb had split in two to again form the wizards' original red and blue lightning bolts. The wizards were aghast with anticipation and eager questions as to what was going on, until the throbbing and restless bolts lined up again and arched towards each other, ready for attack. When finally the bolts rocketed towards each other, the two wizards broke to the side but were too late to avoid being hit by the shock waves that followed when the red and blue streaks crashed together in a gargantuan blast that made everything tremble at once. There was little time to recover before a second explosion went up and a huge disturbance came from the ground beneath Linahen Rock that caused a gaping crack to open and to run from its base to its pinnacle.

Both Garret and Largol, recovering from the first explosion, were again knocked off their feet by the force of the massive new blast. Dartradisadene, too, had been swept off his feet but recovered quickly when he noticed that Aoife was nowhere to be seen. Just then a sweet sound rose above the turmoil, a melodious and lilting cry that made everyone stop to listen. It was Aoife, and she had begun to sing her exquisite, mystical song, a song that was not just a call for the fish to swim again to Lissendel and for her crops to grow but a salutary praise to her shores and her rivers and their maker. She was standing before an alter-like mound at the top of Linahen Rock, her ghostly silhouette shimmering against the ashen light of the moon when Largol, swollen with rage as he rose again to his feet, spotted her. Driven by his disbelief that she was succeeding in singing her song despite all his efforts to stop her, he jumped up and made for the trail that led up to where she was, all the time calling for his men — most of whom had begun to scatter and to run away in fear such was the fierceness of the explosion — to regroup and to renew their attacks.

Garret's recovery from the blasts was much slower than Largol's, but he too could hear Aoife's song and, although drowsy and somewhat incoherent, was aware of Largol's race to stop her from fully completing it. Knowing also, that the natural laws that had been suspended by Largol's devilment could only be put back in place by Aoife's song being sung fully by her to its completion... in that exact place and at that exact time, he stumbled up onto his feet and began his chase to help her. When he reached the top of Linahen Rock Largol was shouting a warning at Aoife while aiming his staff directly at her.

"Stop!" he shouted. "Stop the song now!"

"Leave her!" shouted Garret, realizing just then that in his rush to catch Largol, he had mislaid his own staff.

Largol said nothing but in an instant turned and shot a jagged beam from his staff at Garret that struck him high on the shoulder. Instantly, he went down. The blow from the lightning beam wasn't fatal but was enough to incapacitate a man of Garret's size for a long period had it not been for his tremendous inner strength that pushed his failing limbs onwards and refused to let him give up. For a moment though, he had felt helpless but then fought a terrible pain to rise up again and to stagger towards Largol, only to fall once more after a few miserly steps. Once again though, he rose and went forward, thinking to conjure his magic to stop Largol or even to physically grapple with him, while realizing that he was too weak to do either. It was when he fell down again that it came to him: a single lucid vision of a face familiar to him, a misted countenance that in seconds he realized was that of the leprechaun, Green. Then he heard, whispered, *"Phoulardnacrushnaparteenthomond!"* At once a flash of thoughts crashed through his drowsy mind that eased his pain and bought him hope. He remembered that before Green died he had told him to use the word when all seemed lost, yet in his weakened state, he doubted if he even had the strength to say it, but again, he pushed himself up.

'Phoular...Phoularna...Phoulardnacrushnaparteenthomond!' he wailed finally with a desperate failing breath that brought a staggering weakness on him and caused him to fall once more.

As he went down to his knees, he thought he heard a sound of a great stone sliding back and went to look up, but overwhelmed by the pain that he was experiencing and an ever growing feeling of hopelessness, he closed his eyes despairingly and sank down even lower than before. In that same second, a cold shadow crossed where he lay, and he heard a voice that sounded like Largol's crying, "*No! No!*" Then another shadow followed it that - although he had feared the worst at that penultimate moment – gave him a strange and unexpected warmth that prompted him to look up. More confused than ever, he looked across the open space to where Aoife was and was surprised to see that she was unmoved and still there singing her song. Near her in the alter-like mound from where, he suddenly realized, had come the sound of the great stone sliding back there was a dark doorway and a chasm that had somehow been opened. As his mind became more lucid, his attention switched to the sounds behind him, the sounds of desperate movements and of Largol pleading. Immediately, he turned to see Largol retreating and then cowering sheepishly under an onslaught of pushes and blows that were being meted out by a ghastly giant figure that his magic was useless against.

"Save me! Please! Garret Dimple, save me from this...this monster!" pleaded Largol, swinging his broken staff in an effort to use his magic. "Who is it? What is it? Is it a demon you've conjured up?"

When Garret looked more closely at the giant, he saw both a recognizable face and a spectral shimmer that at once answered Largol's panicked questions. It was the ghost of the giant Andale. He knew then, that it was Green's special word: *Phoulardnacrushnaparteenthomond* that had summoned forth the giant from his grave.

"It is I, Andale," said the giant to Largol. "Do you not remember how I gave up my life at this very place?"

"It can't be you," answered Largol, incredulously. "But you're...you're..."

" – Dead?" Andale answered. "Yes, I'm dead, and beyond the reach of your black magic!"

Largol then tried to scurry away, but whichever way he turned, Andale was there before him. "What do you want with me?" he cried, terrified. "It was the sacrifice required by the song that took your life, not me."

"But you caused it all to happen when you brought down your curse on Lissendel. The same way you've caused it to happen again. But this time the sacrifice is yours! You see, I've come to take you back with me!"

Largol ran to Garret and threw himself at his feet. "Help me! Help me, please! Don't let him take me! I'll leave here forever! The girl can sing her song!"

"I can't help you," said Garret. "I won't..."

Andale was dragging Largol towards the chasm beneath the alter-like mound when Biddy and the children, followed by Dartradisadene (who, together with a group of other captives, had been released from their chains when Largol's ruffians fled following the great explosion) came up from below.

At first Garret couldn't understand why they were all laughing until he realized that Andale was invisible to everyone but him and Largol. Even Aoife was unable to see him. As far as all of them were concerned, Largol's involuntary scamper across the ground was just another example of Garret's powerful magic.

"What's going on?"laughed Sammy.

"Garret's beaten him!" exclaimed Padraig.

Louise, Dervla, and Maeve shouted joyously in support of Garret and speculated about how everyone would celebrate his victory over Largol on their return to Creel, while Dartradisadene, Biddy and her cats seemed somewhat mystified but relieved as they watched Largol, his face contorted with fear, screaming as he was being drawn backwards (as if by some invisible force) to where the alter-like mound was, and then down into its gaping chasm. Under the sweet tones of Aoife's voice, Largol's screams became hollow and more distant, and when the great stone was rolled back to close the chasm, only the alluring cry and call of her song could be heard. Like a sacred string of exquisite prayers, each lilting word cascaded from her

tongue in a gentle wash that was lifted tenderly by the night air
and spread to every corner of Lissendel:

The seasons falling one by one across the land and sea

Are calling to the fish to come, come to our crystal streams,

*The sacred song of the Salmon Girl guides you and
implores,*

*Oh swim again to our silver rivers, come back to our
lonely shores.*

Come, come, come, come, come, come,

Come home to our lonely shores.

*The life that made us what we are came from the tumbling
seas,*

And now we call on you to come, come to set us free.

The land is crying out to you, the moon, the sun, come see,

Your spawning pools are waiting here, dark and silently.

Come, come, come, come, come, come,

Come home and set us free.

*The wind is whispering countless names of those with
broken hearts,*

But hope will always find a way if love can play its part,

Our silver streams are waiting for your coming once again,

Pray never more, oh never more that I sing my song again.

The seasons falling one by one across the land and sea,

Are calling to the fish to come, come to our crystal streams,

The sacred song of the Salmon Girl guides you and implores,

Oh swim again in our silver rivers, come back to our lonely shores.

Come, come, come, come, come, come,

Come home to our lonely shores.

Even when Aoife had stopped singing, the echo of her song went on through the night, its haunting resonance ghosting from valley to valley and from ravine to mountaintop. It was as if there had been some great release and as though, even before daylight peeked over the hills, a dark veil had been lifted from all the lands of Lissendel. When Biddy and the others regrouped, they were so jubilant and thankful at the way everything had turned out that they forgot about Aoife. Only Garret, looking out over the heads of the others who were laughing and dancing with delight while listening to the repeating echoes of Aoife's song across the valleys of Lissendel, was aware enough to wave goodbye to her when she turned a last time towards them with a sad smile before slipping away into the lifting mists of that early morning.

CHAPTER 19

It took only days after Biddy and the children had returned to Creel for the news - that the fish were swimming again to Lissendel's rivers and shores and that the crops would yield a fair harvest - to reach every town and hamlet throughout the land. Everyone had their own interpretation as to what had happened to make it possible, but few knew the true events or appreciated the dangers that had been faced by those who took part in them. Stories abounded, some of which blamed the erratic patterns of the weather as the culprit for the failing crops and for the absence of the fish and then for their reappearance. Other tales played out the story of the warring wizards, mixing half-truth with liberal embellishments and realistic enhancements that, while not far off the truth, served only to make it more palatable to those who had long since stopped believing in magic and things fantastic. The only thing common to all the various stories was that not one of them matched another, but that was the way that things were in those parts. Even the renewed Lissendelian Council, whose twelve members (mostly wise elders from Creel and its surroundings) had been in hiding such was their fear of Largol and his agents, had their own tame versions of the events, but all of them knew the real ones and realized just how lucky an escape that they had had. It was most evident too, when they called boldly for a work-free day throughout the land and for a gargantuan celebration on that day that was as much out of sheer relief to have been freed from Largol's threat as it was to honour the fact that the fish were swimming again and the crops were growing. They called for it to be a festivity like no other in the history of Lissendel, beginning at mid-day with a diverse and colourful pageant through the humped and twisted streets of Creel and out into the lush fields around, where there would be a magnificent banquet waiting for all to enjoy and hours of spectacular entertainment, showing all the delightful artistic talents that came naturally to Lissendelians both above and below ground.

During the days before the celebration, there was a wonderfully agreeable air of expectation in all the people of Creel, but they knew that nothing would compare to the day itself when song and dance and laughter would fill the streets from early morning to late at night. Such was the feeling of goodwill and friendship amongst the townsfolk that all their worry about how they would survive an uncertain future that had plagued them just a short time before then seemed like a distant memory.

"Not only are the fish swimming again," said Jimson Daley, a dumpy fishmonger, to his old friend Francey Bean who was a farmer, as they brushed past Biddy on the bridge into the town early on the day before the festivity, "but there seems to be more of them, and they seem...well, bigger than before!"

"There's somethin' about the land too," answered Francey, stroking his chin happily. "I...I can't quite put my finger on it, but there's...new life to it, you know?"

"I don't believe all the stories though about wizards and little people and that old one they call the witch," continued Jimson. "I mean, it's all a bit far-fetched if you ask me."

"Ah sure, there's been stories about that old witch and the little people and those wizards around these parts for as long as I can remember. This time though, Jim, it's like, well, you can almost feel something in the air."

The fishmonger laughed dismissively. "Go on out of that! You can put everything down to the strange weather we've been having lately: the fish not swimming and the crops wilting. It was all to do with the weather, I tell you!'

"What about the Joe and Marcella O'Sullivan's young girl, Dervla? They say the little people took her while she was out playing up at the fairy rath in Lushly Fields."

"Who are they trying to fool? Sure didn't I see her walking the road back from Lushly Fields, looking bold as brass, the day after they said she went missing!"

"That wasn't her. You see the little people replaced her with a changeling, a hag of some sort that looked like her, so the story goes. It must have been her that you saw."

"A changeling! A hag!" exclaimed Jimson, incredulously. "It just gets more and more fantastic! If you ask me they've been having a good laugh at our expense. I've heard so many stories now that I don't know what to believe."

"Seemingly there was a clash between the two wizards: Largol Despalt and that Garret Dimple fella," explained Francey. "Largol, he's the one from the north, was supposed to have put a curse on Lissendel, and it was that that stopped the fish swimming and that would have in time stopped all the crops growing too."

Jimson coughed with laughter. "Largol Despalt – sure isn't he the one who owns all the land up north? What would he want more land for?"

Francey went on, his voice high-pitched with his eagerness to tell the story. "He wanted to bring us all to our knees and take over the whole of Lissendel. The only way the curse could be lifted was if this special creature, the Salmon Girl, would sing her song at a certain time from the very top of Linahen Rock. The only problem was the Salmon Girl, Aoife is her name, had gone into hiding, and nobody knew where she was, not even the little people. In panic, they took the O'Sullivan girl, Dervla, who you know has a wonderfully gifted singing voice, and replaced her with a changeling. They thought that with such a great voice like hers she would easily master the *Song of the Salmon Girl* and sing it to lift the curse. You see, they depend as much as we do on the fish in our rivers and the crops in our fields. What they didn't know was that no human voice could ever master such a song."

Jimson was still unconvinced. "And what about this other wizard this, Garret Dimple?"

"Garret Dimple got involved to help get the O'Sullivan girl back from the little people. Largol and he had avoided each other for a long long time, neither wanting to test the patience of the other, and knowing that if they ever came face to face the question as to who was the more powerful would be almost unavoidable. But this whole affair brought them on a collision course. The outcome of it all saw the Salmon Girl finally singing her song and Largol's defeat at the hands of Garret Dimple. I'm sure there's more to the story but that's all I've heard."

"They found the real Salmon Girl then, is what your sayin'?"

"Yes. And the singing of her song lifted the curse, but not before the two wizards lambasted each other!"

"As I said before, it gets more and more fantastic!" laughed Jimson. "And I don't believe a word of it!"

Biddy smiled wryly as she listened to them talking. She knew that there must be other such conversations going on everywhere throughout Creel and soon they would be going on throughout the length and breadth of Lissendel. There had always been a sense of wonder and magic about the history of Lissendel and always believers and those who chose not to.

As if all her senses had been intensified, Biddy heard and noticed everything that went on as she made her way through Creel that day: the robust laugher coming from unseen men in the Rough Baker bakery store and the smell the bread baking; the whistling of the milkman and the clip-clop of his horse and the rolling of the wheels on his cart; the calls to try and to buy coming from the women on the market stalls on Low Street; and the pungent smell of the vegetable market further on where more cries to try and to buy went up. All around her there was movement in and out of the town's colourful doors and up and down its maze of cobbled streets. Men, women, and children were everywhere, coming and going, buying for the party and gathering for it. For a moment, Biddy just stopped and closed her eyes and listened to it all. To her, it was a delicate and beautiful symphony of the noise of every activity of everyone in Creel, something that could have been taken away had things turned out differently but, that because of the sacrifice and selflessness of a few had been preserved.

When Biddy returned to her house in the woods that night, she had just time to feed her cats, Penny and Pinch, and to sip a bowl of her herb and vegetable soup that she had prepared that morning before she left, before a weighty tiredness came down on her which made her seek the comfort of her rocking chair by the fireplace where she began to fall asleep. For minutes, she tried to fight a tugging tiredness; yawning and mumbling about how strangely jaded she felt before dismissing this as an effect of all the journeying she had done in the previous days. Then, with her words faltering in a rambling gabble and her mind becoming almost incoherent, she called out several things she needed to do before she could allow herself to go to sleep, but hardly had their names left her lips when she slipped into a deep, deep slumber. Once asleep her mind was inundated with a million images of high dark mountains and lush valleys and rushing rivers and tumbling seas. It was as if she was flying over them all and swooping high and low with the grace of some majestic eagle. It seemed too, that she was searching for something, but for what, she was unable to tell. Suddenly, below her there was a clearing, a vast wasteland that was spread out around a high broken mountain in an immeasurable span that stretched as far as her eyes could see. It would have only been a short time before, she thought, that the whole valley floor had been laid bare by some immense acrid explosion from the still smoking mountain, and yet, while there was no signs of life, she began to sense that there was still some there. Moments after, she swooped down closer to the valley's floor as a flashing light near its centre shone brilliantly towards her, as if to beckon her to land. In another second, she found that not only had she landed but that she was also walking towards the mysterious light.

"A shadow lost in a million shadows," said a voice.

"I don't understand," Biddy answered.

"This is the realm of shadows, a Hades of cruel anguish for those who walk the land shadow-less. I've brought you here to give you a warning."

Biddy shook her head in disbelief. "This is a dream. I'm asleep and dreaming. That's all."

"No! No! No!" exclaimed the voice with a thunderous quake. "Listen to my voice. Do you not recognize an old friend?"

"An old friend?" repeated Biddy.

"A shadow of an old friend, then," said the voice before it came forward to reveal a shimmering resemblance to Garret Dimple.

Biddy could only stutter. "Gar-ret, is th-at you?"

"I'm his shadow, his better part," laughed the voice fiendishly.

"But what do you want with me?"

"Already my ex-owner is making plans to come here to take me back. Tell him not to bother! I belong to another. It would be, let's say, unhealthy for him to come here."

"But with no shadow he's growing weak," pleaded Biddy. "A wizard without his shadow is—"

"Not a wizard anymore!" interjected the shadow, finishing what Biddy was about to say. "As he grows weak I grow strong. As his powers falter, mine thrive and develop. Soon there will be only one Garret Dimple, and he'll be here in the realm of the shadows where human weakness has no place."

Biddy snapped angrily. "If you think Garret will accept this, you don't know him!"

Suddenly, red streaks glowed in the shadow where its eyes would have been, and a shout came back at Biddy that was as cold and malevolent as it was calculated. "I'm his shadow, remember! He can't destroy me without destroying himself. Whereas I, having being released from the bondage of walking with him, can choose to bring an end to his days without ending my own."

"What evil is behind this? What abomination turned you against your master?"

"All will be revealed in time, but not now." answered the shadow as an icy coldness fell around Biddy.

"You've been poisoned by some magic! Is it the race of the Mawlingfer that you serve now?"

"I've been freed, that's all," laughed the shadow callously. "So tell the old wizard to keep away from these parts, if he knows what's good for him!"

Biddy went to plead and to protest again but was suddenly sucked backwards through a dark vortex with a great jolt that made her shudder and cry for help. It was then she heard another voice that she recognized immediately. It was Garret Dimple.

"Are you okay, Biddy? Are you?" he asked with a voice that had none of the malice that had been present in the voice of his shadow.

"I'm back! I'm home!" she said, looking around as if surprised that she had somehow been returned to her own home and was still sitting in her rocking chair by the fireplace.

"I let myself in," said Garret, his eyes evaluating Biddy's obvious confusion. "Did you not hear me knocking? Is there something wrong, Biddy?"

"One minute I was here sleeping and the next I was..." came her bewildered reply. Then breathless with the sudden realization of where she had been and what she had seen and the warning that she had been given for Garret, she started to tell him all that had happened, and while explaining that it could have been a dream, but that if it was, it was one of a most strange and vivid nature. She added that they both knew never to fully dismiss or to take such portentous dreams lightly.

Sometime after, Biddy was again set-on by tiredness and drifted off to sleep once more, mumbling repeated warnings to Garret as he covered her with a blanket. There had been so many questions she wanted to ask him, but when she woke the next morning, he was already gone.

Later that morning, she trekked back into Creel for the celebrations. Even on the outskirt of the town, the noise of the festivities were robust and jovial with drummers leading a dancing pageant that trailed from street to street as if to wake all the late sleepers and to encourage those who had had second thoughts about joining in the fun to come and take part. Further on, there were variety acts such as children's magicians and clowns, some of which would join forces to create both laughter and magic in the very same instance. There were brightly clad high-rope walkers and somersault performers whose balance and agility seemed to defy the laws of gravity. There were groups of highly skilled jumpers and tumblers travelling the streets in a froglike train while skipping and leaping and a line of exotic dancers from the town of Fansil in eastern Lissendel (commissioned specially for the celebration) following on, clanging cymbals and ringing bells. And while there had been great crowds all along the way it was in the centre of Creel, where there were even entertainers to entertain the entertainers that the greatest crowd had gathered. Throughout the day the festivities went on without pause or mishap. Always there was a new entertainment to replace one that had gone before so that everyone, even those performing, had time to enjoy themselves.

As evening approached, Dartradisadene, who had happily watched the goings on in Creel throughout the day from a cloaked disguise, decided that it was time he made his way back to Bunkleen Mount where he knew King Lugh had planned a similar celebration. Only Biddy had been aware of his presence in the crowd and understood that it would have been detrimental for him to walk openly amongst them, even though he had been of considerable help in the defeat of Largol and a true stalwart warrior for the cause of the Salmon Girl singing her song. Although the worlds of those above ground and those below it touched one another, they were always meant to exist apart. Yet still, Biddy couldn't help but feel a little sadness when she saw him slinking off alone and would have loved to have called him back to join in with their celebrations. Instead, she made her mind up never to let him be forgotten (for she knew that to the little people to be forgotten was a death in itself) and to seek him out in the future as a true friend.

Later that evening in the main square, there were even more entertainers but these were mostly singers and those with rare musical talents whom, because of their special gifts, were kept in waiting for the build up to the celebratory speeches that had been planned and the great banquet that would follow in the surrounding streets and fields. When the first of the singers had sung there was a planned pause after which Bill Weaselbie, the president of the Lissendelian Council, climbed the steps onto a presentation stand near where Biddy and the children were standing. Then, following several introductory coughs to convey that he would soon begin his speech, he stepped up on a podium and coughed a little louder than before. Immediately, the word "Hush" travelled through the crowd from one person to the next, until there was almost total silence.

"We pause to acknowledge great events," he said, causing a cheer from the back of the crowd. "Ones that not only have taken a great threat away from the future but that have even helped to shape it! I don't need to tell you all about the dark days that we've been through. Days that proffered nothing but poverty, famine and death, and an endless trek into the unknown for those few of our blessed people who would have survived these terrible admonitions. Days where they would have had no option but to take to the roads and seas in search of new lives in the desolation of the uncharted places. Truly, they would have been days of doom where the living would have envied the dead! But now I can tell you that those days are over and that that particular threat that hung over us for so long has been removed forever! But never let that threat be forgotten! Was it an act of nature, some disturbance of the seasons, or was it caused by something more devious? We may never know for sure. And never let it be forgotten either that we have proven ourselves to be a strong people who have stood together through thick and thin to boldly face and overcome that threat." Again, cheers and hurrahs and whistles went up, but Biddy and the children just shook their heads to one another in disbelief, for they knew that all of those on the Lissendelian Council knew exactly what had caused the fish to stop swimming and the crops to fail, and each one of them had been given explicit details by them of how the whole affair had been resolved.

"Yes, there will be other threats," continued the speech. "Threats great and small, and not just to each one of us but to us all! Perhaps a great storm will come down on us in the dead of night, or the seas will flood our shores. The seasons are uncontrollable and may sometimes bring disaster to our doors, but together we can make provision for these mishaps and overcome the burdens they bring. Only together can we do this. But what if the danger came from folk like us? What if it came from within our own borders by those who would have us all serve and bow down before them? Maybe the threat will come from some outsiders who lurk even now within this crowd. Many outsiders view our lands with avaricious eyes and would have us all under their thumb, if we let them, but we'll never let them! The events we celebrate are the continuance of our traditions and our ways. The fish are swimming again, and the crops are going to be rich and abundant! We are a people who will go on, who will thrive and continue without change or upheaval! But have no doubt that more threats will come, more dark days will follow, and more shadows will cover our lands! We know we are a sacred people, but so do others! Before long, they'll come to entice us with modern gadgets and grand schemes, while all the time hiding the true malignant and treacherous nature of their plans! That is why we must always be a people who will stand up bravely in the face of adversary for the preservation of our old ways. Change is unnecessary! Change is not good! Change is an evil!" Then turning to Biddy and the children, with a reflex acknowledgement that he quickly disguised, he went on. "How many amongst us would be protectors of our ways? We of the Lissendelian Council have borne the weight of the scourges that have plagued our land so you don't have to. On your behalf, I thank the Council for their dedication and their bravery."

"Will you listen to that liar," complained Biddy to the children, as again the crowd raised their voices with cheers and hurrahs.

Before continuing again, Bill Weaselbie smiled and nodded to the other members of the Lissendelian Council who were all now lined up at the side of the podium to give their own speeches. "We know too," he resumed, "from the reports that we've had that there are others who should be thanked, but who for reasons unknown, cannot be present here with us today."

"We should be thanked," said Sammy quietly to the others.

"And Garret Dimple and Dartradisadene too," added Louise.

Suddenly, Padraig shouted. "I never saw anyone from the Lissendelian Council doing anything worthwhile ever!"

But his voice was drowned out by that of Bill Weaselbie when he suddenly raised his. "Today we celebrate their victory! And thank them with all our hearts! We, the Lissendelian Council, give you this celebration of celebrations in honour of the prodigious continuance of our ways and traditions. Now everyone, let's celebrate!"

Biddy and the children were astounded at the extent of the rumbustious clapping and cheering that followed from the crowd. For a moment when Sammy was looking out over the smoke of the celebrations, he thought he saw a silhouette of a man against the skyline of the Treefellwells Hills. When he told the others, they searched for the figure but were unable to see anything until a flash grew in the sky above those same dark hills, forming fiery letters which read, *Farewell my friends!*

"Look, it's from Garret!" said Biddy.

"Why doesn't he come and join in the celebration?" Sammy asked. "He should get all the credit!"

"As long as I've known Garret, he's always been one to shy away from taking credit for any of his heroics. He's always been like that, and he always will be. Even if he wanted to join us, I doubt if he'd have the time. If my guess is right, he'll be travelling far off now to search for his shadow. He'll have a whole set of new problems to worry about and many new battles to fight."

THE END

Now follow the continuing adventures of Garret Dimple in:

GARRET DIMPLE AND THE CURSE OF THE SHADOWTAKERS